OUT OF GOMORRAH

A TALE OF COYOTES, POLLOS, AND RESILIENCE.

A STORY OF THE BORDERLANDS

ROBERT C MARSETT

RANGES Press

Tucson, Arizona
A division of RANGES LLC

First printing 2025
The characters and events in this book are fictional, and any resemblance to actual persons or events is coincidental.

ISBN-13: 978-0-9841030-3-4
ISBN-10: 0-9841030-3-1

For the victims of human trafficking.

CHAPTER ONE

Cochise County, Arizona, June 1995

The cowboy was prowling the western edge of the ranch in a pasture bordering a public road. His prowling was as much about having a visible presence as it was to check on the cattle and the waters. It was Sunday, the other cowboys' day off. He liked it like this. He was not an introvert. He did, in fact, like the company of others, but Sundays were his opportunity to be alone. On Sundays, he had no questions to field, no decisions to make, and no telephones to answer. Sundays were about clearing his mind by remembering what he'd learned from his Uncle Jack. It's a ranch, they're cows. Tomorrow it'll still be a ranch, and they'll still be cows. You're not defending the Constitution of the United States. Enjoy being a cowboy." The cowboy reined in his horse, looked at the spectacular landscape surrounding him, and marveled at his good luck. He silently thanked God, or at least his personal notion of God, for his wife, his family, and his life.

As he approached the windmill at Alice Well, he could see the cattle were bunched up at the open gate to the water lot. They were agitated, holding their heads high and looking towards the drinker. They wanted to go in for their daily drink of water, but something had them spooked.

The cowboy let out a sigh. This could only mean trouble. He pushed forward, slapping his quirt against his chaps to encourage the cows to move out of his way. He expected to find a dead or injured bovine turned turtle in the drinker, something he knew would require a lot of heavy work to remedy. As he rode forward, there was a slight breeze in his face, and he caught the sickening, sweet smell that could only mean one thing: a dead critter. "Shit," he said under his breath, it was going to be smelly as well as hard work.

His horse had started to wring his tail and blow rolls. This was not normal behavior for Tadpole, a seasoned cow horse that had seen his share of dead animals. The horse's uneasiness became the cowboy's uneasiness. He reined Tadpole to a stop, hung his quirt over the saddle horn, and scanned the area. Stepping down from his horse, he eased his pistol from its holster.

Dropping the reins to the ground, he moved forward carefully. A bunch of Ravens flew up from the water lot. That was no surprise; they were often the first to find a meal of carrion.

As he entered the water lot, he saw a small, pink backpack on the ground. Its contents had been dumped out and scattered, as if someone had rifled through them. There were baby bottles, baby clothes, unused diapers, and women's underwear.

He dropped into a crouch. With his head on a swivel, the cowboy cautiously moved further into the water lot, checking his surroundings for anything out of place. Approaching the drinker, a rectangular concrete trough, he could see there were no legs poking out of it towards the sky, which was the norm for a cow that had fallen in and died.

He stopped and slowly straightened up, peering over the drinker, and he saw the body lying in the dust. Dropping to a knee, he rechecked his surroundings, determining it was clear, he stood up and holstered his pistol.

He approached the corpse, and looking down at the half-naked body of a young woman, the cowboy removed his hat and dropped his head in a short prayer. As he turned away from the woman, he replaced his hat, started back towards his horse, and said, "Well, Tadpole, let's get back to headquarters."

After pushing the cows back and closing the gate to the water lot, Bob Hasett looked at the cows and said, "Sorry, girls, I can't have you in there right now. He swung up into his saddle and put Tadpole into a high trot.

They should cover the eight miles back to the Tres Cruces Ranch headquarters in under an hour. He had to get word to the Sheriff about the dead woman in his West Pasture. As he rode back to headquarters, Bob kept wondering what he had just seen. A partially undressed dead woman seemed straightforward enough; some sick bastard had raped and killed her, but the backpack, baby clothes, and baby bottles were out of place. Then the unsettling question: Where was the baby?

+++

When Bob reached the ranch headquarters, he found His headquarters cowboy, Jim, relaxing outside the bunkhouse on his Sunday off. Bob apologized for interfering with his free time and asked him to unsaddle Tadpole and turn him out, "I hate to ask, but time is short," he said. "As soon as I call the sheriff, you and I are headed to Alice Well. We'll take the Bronco. Be sure it's got plenty of gas and throw one of those blue tarps and a bunch of baling twine in the back. We could be there for a while."

As they were driving back to Alice Well, Bob explained what he had found. They turned off the road at the gate to West Pasture. It was a three-mile, bumpy ride from there to the well.

When they reached Alice Well, Bob and Jim rigged the blue tarp to shade the Body. It was the least they could do. He and Jim had been careful not to touch anything from the backpack, and they had tried to leave as few of their footprints as possible. Bob sent Jim back to the gate to wait for the sheriff's deputy. He figured the deputy could find the gate, but he had no faith in his finding the water lot at Alice Well.

Bob was waiting in the shade of the cottonwoods that were a fixture at most water points in this part of the world. The flats, east of the Chiricahua Mountains, comprised the western part of Tres Cruces Ranch. They were a mix of semi-arid grasslands and Chihuahua Desert shrubs.

The stunted mesquite, white-thorn acacia, and creosote that were scattered over this dry landscape provided pretty sorry shade. Aside from a few large drainages with significant stands of riparian vegetation, the cottonwoods at the isolated water points provided the only other refuge from the summer sun.

Bob climbed partway up the windmill tower to the pipe that spilled water into the holding tank. There was just enough wind to turn the blades and pump a little water. Bob unclipped the enameled coffee cup from the tower, held it under the spill pipe, filled it, and drank.

Then he held his wrists under the pipe, soaking the cuffs of his shirt, after which he poured water on his collar. It was an old trick to soak the cloth at the wrist and neck, those places where blood ran near the surface. Cool the blood, cool the body, he had been told as a teenager. Once finished, he replaced the cup. All the wells and springs on Tres Cruces had cups like this.

Rather than climb down right away, he looked across the countryside. It was open, and it was hot. Only a mile or two to his west were a few ancient andesitic volcanic cones, not more than a few hundred feet high. Looking past them, the heat waves caused distant objects to shimmer. This time of day, in the summer heat, nothing with a brain was moving. Even the thirsty cows waiting to get a drink had sought whatever paltry shade they could find and were standing still or lying down.

The only movement was a distant dust devil meandering across the valley floor.

Starting about twenty-five miles away, across the valley, were several mountain ranges, stretching off into the distance. They seemed to be stacked on one another, going on and on, forever. Bob knew many people considered this border country of deserts and scattered mountain ranges to be the middle of nowhere, but he knew different. It was home.

A memory flooded into Bob's mind. He remembered a view very much like this from over twenty years ago. It had been cold then, not hot. There were no dust devils, and there were even fewer trees, but the expansive vistas were the same, the majesty was the same, and the solitude was the same. Instead of rattlesnakes and scorpions, there had been grizzly bears and wolves. Instead of killing heat for the unaware, there was freezing cold for the unprepared. Once, he had thought of that place as the middle of nowhere, yet some called the North Slope of Alaska home. From one such, he had learned to be happy there.

His thoughts were interrupted by the dust of a vehicle coming up the road from the valley. He hoped it was the sheriff. The dust stopped where Bob knew the gate to West Pasture was. After a few minutes, the dust resumed heading his way at a much slower speed. Soon Bob could see the ranch Bronco and a Sheriff's pickup approaching. It was time to climb down and get to business.

Bob was standing at the gate to the water lot waiting on Jim and the Deputy. The cows seemed to be watching him hopefully. "Not yet, girls," Bob said to the cows.

"Howdy, Bob," said Tommy Judson.

"Howdy, Tommy," Bob answered. Looking at Tommy's uniform collar, Bob said, "It appears congratulations are in order, Lieutenant Judson."

Tommy laughed, held out his hand, and said, "I waited them out. The boss decided that since I wasn't leaving, he had no choice but to promote me."

Bob replied, "I'm sure you earned it long ago." Then, pointing towards the drinker, Bob asked, "Are you ready?"

"Yeah, let's go see what's up."

After a cursory check of the body, Tommy walked back over to where Bob was standing in the shade. "I need to get word back to the office to send an investigator out here. I have a radio in my truck."

"Should I send Jim back to the gate?" asked Bob.

"Let's see what they have to say first."

Tommy contacted his office and was told to conduct the initial investigation and collect the evidence himself. It would be turned over to the General Crime Team in the morning.

When Tommy had explained, they would need to transport the body sooner rather than later, he was told someone from the funeral home would be out to pick it up. Tommy said to Bob, "The funeral home is sending someone for the body. You should probably send your cowboy back to wait on them."

Tommy had A-frame-shaped numbered tags, a camera, and evidence bags. He placed a numbered tag next to each item of interest and then photographed it. He took several photos of the body and the overall scene, even climbing up the windmill tower to get an overall view. When he was done, he filled out some cards describing each of the items he had photographed, linking them to the corresponding tags by number and marking an evidence bag with the same number for each, then bagging the items.

After Tommy had finished gathering the evidence, he and Bob were sitting in the shade of the cottonwoods, waiting. They had seen the dust of a vehicle driving towards the West Pasture gate from the valley. It would be a while before it got to Alice Well. Tommy asked, "How is everything on Tres Cruces?"

"It's all going pretty well. Stepping in to fill Uncle Jack's boots was a bit daunting, but he took such good care of the place that it was just a case of continuing the same operation. You know the old saying. If it ain't broke, don't fix it."

"Yeah, but not everyone gets it."

Bob smiled at Tommy. "That's because everyone is looking to put another feather in their war bonnet. When someone's put in a new position of authority, they are asked, What are you going to do? What changes are you going to make to improve the operation? Damn few are willing to say I'm changing nothing, it's all going well.

"It sounds like you've had experience with this."

"Don't get me started." Said Bob.

Tommy seemed to be thinking about something. Finally, he said, "Bob, you went back into the army, yet you always kept your iron in the fire with this place. You came back year after year to help Jack with the Spring or Fall works. Folks around here remember that."

"After all Uncle Jack and Aunt Maria did for my family, how could I do less? "Besides," Bob added with a smile, "while I loved soldering, it was a pleasure to get away from the army from time to time."

Tommy asked, "How is your family, Bob?"

"They are all doing well. We'll have to have you over for dinner sometime to catch up." Bob pointed at the dust to the south, "They're coming." With that, the two men walked back over to the gate.

Jim drove up in the Bronco. He stepped out of the vehicle and walked up to Tommy and Bob, carrying a folded body bag. "The funeral home sent a hearse. It can't make it from the gate to hear." Holding out the body bag towards Tommy, he continued. "They asked if you could bring them the body."

"OK," said Tommy. "I was hoping they would be here for this part. I need to ask you two to help me. I have to check her more closely for injuries. We have to roll her over and get some more photos. After that, we can put her in the body bag and load her into the bed of my truck. I'm sorry, I was hoping to spare you from this."

Bob looked at Tommy and said, "It's alright, she's not my first. We're glad to help." Then, turning to Jim, he said, "Right?"

Jim wasn't sure about this, but he knew the correct answer. "Yes, sir, that's right."

She was lying face down with her jeans on the ground nearby and her panties twisted around one ankle. There was a dark area in the dirt that spread from under her. Tommy stood close to the body, pointed at the ground on either side of him, and said, "Stand here next to me. We will roll her over towards us." As they rolled her over onto her back, the putrid smell of decay wafted out even stronger than before. With that, Jim rushed away and lost his breakfast.

Bob and Tommy stood looking down at the body. She was partially eviscerated. "Oh, no," said Tommy. He was having a hard time controlling his temper. "She's just a kid. What animal does this?"

Bob answered, "The two-legged, fucked up, sad sack of shit kind."

Tommy shot a look of disapproval at Bob. Bob saw it and said, "You may be a practicing Mormon in good standing with the church, but I'm not." Casting a look at the dead girl, he said. "Scum bags that do this shit deserve whatever title I choose to give them."

"It's your soul," said Tommy.

"Yep, that it is, and I put it in serious jeopardy long ago. If God's not the forgiving kind, I'm already screwed. Now let's get back to the task at hand."

Tommy checked her over closely. He thought she'd been dead for a couple of days. The bugs and ravens had been at her, but not the big scavengers like coyotes and vultures. She had long black hair and a trim build. Her eyes might have been brown, but it was hard to tell. Around her neck was a small chain partially hidden inside her blouse. Tommy pulled it out. There was a medallion. It was Our Lady of Guadalupe. "She's Mexicana," said Tommy.

"Sure, looks that way," said Bob.

Tommy got back to work, examining her more closely and taking more photos. He finished and said, "Not only was she cut open, she also had her throat slit. This is a murder." Then, pointing at her, he asked. "Can you and Jim get her into the body bag while I get the truck ready and bring it over?"

"Of course," answered Bob. Then he looked at Jim, who was bent over by the fence, and called out. "Jim, when you're up to it, come give me a hand."

Bob placed the body bag next to the young woman. He placed the loops of intestine that had pushed out of her wound onto her abdomen before pulling her blouse down over her waist, doing what he could for the woman's modesty. When Jim came back, he was able to help Bob lift her and place her in the body bag and zip it shut. "I'm sorry," said Jim. "I've never seen anything like that."

"It's OK, Jim. You have nothing to be sorry for. At least you know your humanity is still intact."

With that, Jim looked at Bob quizzically. "You and the deputy did OK."

"Not as OK as you might think." Bob looked at the body bag. "Keep your innocence, boy. Hang onto it as long as you can."

+++

Bob was riding in Tommy's pickup, and Jim was following in the ranch Bronco. They were headed to the sheriff's office in Bisbee, where Bob and Jim would give their official statements. Tommy had asked Bob to ride with him. He said he wanted to catch up on the past twenty years.

Bob asked, "Tommy, do you remember the first time we met?"

Tommy thought about it for a minute and then smiled. "Yeah, I remember. It was over by Elfrida on the highway. I was parked on the side of the road in a patrol car. You were in the truck with Jack Barnes, and you saluted me with a beer as you drove by."

"Yes, I did, and you let it pass."

"I let it pass because your Uncle Jack was an outstanding member of this community, and he vouched for you."

"That was September of '71. It seems like a lifetime ago."

"You weren't a local boy. What brought you here?" asked Tommy.

"I had spent summers on the Tres Cruces as a kid. I needed some time to spin down after Vietnam, and I figured cowboying for Uncle Jack would give me a chance to decompress."

"Did it?"

"It did. Cowboying helped me to unwind. Once, when I was getting stressed over some cattle getting away from me, Uncle Jack said, 'Don't stress over this. An honest day's work is all I ask.' That was a big help."

Tommy said, "Everyone around here was sorry about Angelina."

Bob stared ahead at the road. "I don't doubt that. She was a popular young woman."

Tommy said tentatively, "I'm sorry we never caught her killers."

"Yeah, I was pretty pissed with the whole bunch of you. Did you guys ever figure out where the leak was coming from?"

"Yeah, it was a clerk in the County Attorney's Office."

Bob waited for more, but didn't get it, so then he asked. "And?"

"We couldn't prove anything. Everyone from Indian Springs disappeared into thin air. You can't prove someone leaked information if there is no one to leak it to." Then Tommy asked Bob. "You wouldn't know anything about their disappearance, would you?"

"Whose disappearance?" Bob asked.

"Those gangster wannabe cowboys at Indian Springs."

Bob answered coolly. "No, all I know is those dudes failed at ranching, sold out to Uncle Jack, and hauled ass back to New Jersey, or whatever cesspool they crawled out of. You already know that."

Tommy didn't look convinced. "So, the story goes." Then pointedly, "You think they killed Angelina, don't you?"

Bob was getting tired of the game. "Look, Tommy, if you've got something to ask, then spit it out. We've known each other far too long to play games."

"Will you ever tell me what happened back then?"

"Those assholes killed Angelina. I hung around for six months waiting for some justice from the system. You guys couldn't catch them, so there wasn't any. I left and went to Alaska. That's what happened. You know all that." Said Bob.

"Yes, but there's more?"

"You're right, in Alaska, I met Diane, we moved back here, we got married, I went back into the army, had a career, we raised our kids. When Jack died, I retired and took over the ranch. That about covers the last twenty-plus years."

Tommy said. "I know you're not telling me everything about the Indian Springs bunch. I'm not looking to get you in trouble. That bunch all deserved whatever they got. I just want to know."

"There is no Indian Springs bunch. It's all Tres Cruces now." Bob said nothing more.

CHAPTER TWO

Cochise County, Arizona, July 1995

Tommy Judson had called Bob and asked for a meeting. He wanted to share what they had learned about the young woman Bob had found at Alice Well. As it turned out, Bob had to be at the Forest Service office in Douglas the next morning, so they agreed to meet for lunch.

Bob was waiting at Dos Hermanas, a small restaurant right next to the border fence in Douglas. It was best known for its albondigas, or meatball soup in English. He hoped the strained atmosphere of their last encounter a month ago would not prevail. Tommy walked in and came to the table. Bob stood and offered Tommy his hand. "How are you, Lieutenant Judson?"

Tommy smiled and said, "It's like that, is it, Mr. Hasett?"

With an overblown air of dignitas, Bob responded. "It's Sergeant Major Hasett, or as my kids call me, El Magnifico."

"Were you really a Sergeant Major?"

Bob maintained his air of false dignity and said, "No, but I played one in my imagination."

Having lightened the mood, they ordered lunch.

Tommy started by telling Bob the people involved with the case had taken to calling the dead girl, our Pollita, our little chicken, pollos being the coyote's name for their clients. It seemed better than that dead girl, or Jane Doe. They had not been able to identify the body. What they did know was that she was a teenager, fifteen to eighteen years old, and the cause of death was exsanguination due to the slit throat. The disemboweling was postmortem. She'd been dead two or three days when they found her.

The label on her blouse was in Spanish, reading "Hecho en Mexico." The labels on the baby clothes and the pack were also in Spanish, and some New Peso coins were in her pockets. When you add the Our Lady of Guadalupe medallion that she wore around her neck, it's a good guess she's Mexican. Here's the big surprise: she had never given birth. The baby articles were not hers. There must have been at least one other woman with her."

Then Tommy asked, "I know the gate through the fence is a few miles away, but Schellenberger Road passes pretty close to the well."

"Yeah, less than a half mile west of the well. There is a pull-off with a wildcat road that the kids use to park and drink beer. It runs up right next to my fence, about two hundred yards from the well."

Tommy asked, "Is it an easy walk from the well to the fence?"

"Yep, it's a slight downhill grade on a big cow trail from the well to the fence. Are you thinking it's smuggling?"

"Maybe. That's something I need to start looking into, but I'm not officially on the case; the General Crimes Unit has it."

Bob asked. "Is that a good thing?"

"Yeah, it's what they do, but there's more to this than one young lady's death. The Sheriff has asked me to poke around. After I finish here, I'm headed over to the Border Patrol office and see what they think."

Bob gave Tommy a knowing look. "Of course, you didn't prod the old man into letting you work on this."

Tommy answered, "Maybe a little. He said I could do it as long as it didn't interfere with my normal duties."

"Does that mean on your own time?" Asked Bob.

"I'm afraid so."

Can I go with you to the Border Patrol Office?"

"Sure, if you behave."

+++

Bob followed Tommy as they headed west on Highway 191. Funny, Bob thought, for years, Highway 191 was actually Highway 666. That was something of a thorn in the side of some who referred to it as the devil's highway or the beast's highway. Bob smiled to himself; it seemed somebody was always prepared to be offended. During the short drive, he couldn't help but think of the fact that the dead girl was not a mother. The baby clothes, bottles, and diapers belonged to someone else. That added a new wrinkle to what little he thought he knew.

Bob and Tommy were waiting in the Border Patrol Station while the office administrator notified her boss that he had visitors. Soon, Ivan Gomez, the Patrol Agent in Charge of the Douglas Station, came out. He recognized Tommy right away, shook his hand, and asked, "What can the Border Patrol do for the Sheriff's Office?"

Tommy introduced Bob, then gave Gomez the executive summary of what they knew about the death of the girl at Alice Well. The agent responded by saying, "Tommy, let's continue this in my office. Bob, you'll need to wait here."

Tommy spoke up and said, "Bob needs to come in. I can explain in your office."

The agent didn't look pleased but relented. "OK, but if we start getting into sensitive information, I'm going to have to ask him to step out."

"Fair enough."

After explaining what the Sheriff's Office knew, Tommy said, "You and I both know there's change taking place over the border, mass killings outside Agua Prieta, shootouts between cartels and the police in Cananea. Is it about to get bad around here like it is in Juarez?"

Gomez hesitated to answer, then hemmed and hawed awhile using lots of words but saying nothing. When he stopped, the silence got long and awkward. After what seemed like an extremely long time, Bob broke the silence and said, with a note of irritation. "We all know that Operation Hold the Line almost shut down the illicit border traffic in El Paso, and that Operation Gate Keeper is doing the same thing in San Diego. All that traffic has to go somewhere. Is it here? Is that what we stumbled across on my ranch? Are we about to be overrun with smugglers and coyotes running drugs and illegal aliens through here?"

Gomez looked a little shocked and just stared at Bob for a few seconds, then asked, "How do you know any of that?"

"It's not exactly classified. The basics have been released to the press." Seeing that that was not enough for Gomez, Bob continued, "I was with JTF Six for a few years."

Agent Gomez looked uncomfortable. Bob took the hint and said, "Tommy, I'll wait outside."

Gomez stood and shook Bob's hand. "It was nice to meet you."

Bob answered, "My pleasure."

Once the door closed, Gomez asked Tommy, "Is he for real?"

Tommy shrugged and answered, "I don't know. It wouldn't surprise me. He retired from the army last year and spent time at Fort Huachuca. I can find out."

"OK, please find out about JTF Six. What's his connection with you?"

"We go back more than twenty years. He's Jack Barnes' nephew."

Gomez said, "That's before my time here. I do remember that big funeral last year for a rancher, I think his name was Barnes."

Tommy answered, "Yeah, that was him."

"He must have been a big deal around here for that many people to pay their respects."

Tommy said, "He was a big deal and a good man."

"Is this nephew of his like him?"

"He might be. Filling Jack Barnes' boots is a tall order. I do know he's got sand, and I believe he's honest. Jack thought highly of him."

Gomez said, "Well, on to the business at hand. I've been talking with my Customs Service counterpart. What I'm going to tell you now is a compilation of what we are seeing. It is not for public release. You need to keep what I tell you under wraps. The higher-ups get nervous about this stuff. They're overly sensitive to any negative press, which makes them appear bad. Since you already seem to be involved, I had better tell you what I know so you'll have an idea of what's going on, or at least as much as we can discern. I'll contact the Sheriff and fill him in as well."

"OK, Ivan."

Patrol Agent in Charge Ivan Gomez proceeded to tell Tommy Judson about the chaos across the border. Most of what he said to Tommy was common knowledge amongst the border area law enforcement community, but much of what he said was new to Tommy.

Gomez explained how the demise of the Guadalajara Cartel had led to warfare between the rival factions in Mexico, resulting in an enormous amount of bloodshed south of the border. Some in the US counter-narcotics world whispered that the current situation was worse than when the individual cartels and plazas were organized and controlled by Felix Gallardo. At least there was some order then. Now there was only chaos.

Until a year ago, most of the cross-border traffic was managed by the Juarez and Tijuana cartels. Now it was changing. Other players are getting involved, and we don't know who. Gomez confirmed that Bob's fears were founded. The cross-border traffic of illegals at Juarez had been reduced dramatically, and it appeared the operation in San Diego was choking off that sector as well. While these operations were focused on countering the smuggling of drugs, not illegal aliens, the effect on the crossing of illegals was severe. The drugs and the illegals had to cross somewhere. That somewhere was here.

The Border Patrol was now seeing more drugs and illegals coming across the remote stretches of the border. Drug tunnels had been found crossing under the border from Agua Prieta into Douglas. Every time they found one and closed it, another would turn up. As for illegal aliens, in the past they came in ones and twos; now they are being brought across in groups by paid guides called coyotes.

"Tommy," said Agent Gomez. "From what you have told me, it sounds like this young lady could have been part of a group being smuggled across. Where she was found is close enough to a road to be a pickup point. A truck or van could easily transport a load of illegals from there to Tucson or Phoenix," Gomez said, looking at the map on the wall. "That well is over thirty miles from the border; it's too far to walk. They must have a shuttle system set up."

"Who has a shuttle set up, the illegals?"

"No, the coyotes."

Gomez continued. "This large-scale smuggling of human beings is not unheard of, but until now it was uncommon; now it's on the rise. We know almost nothing about these new players, and that bothers me. Things are changing, and I don't like it." Gomez then looked at Tommy and said, "I need to get with your boss. We need to talk all this over. It's time for us to cooperate more."

Tommy said, "I'll pass this on to the Sheriff. Thanks for all the information. Maybe we can get ahead of what's coming."

"God, I hope so." Said Gomez.

When Tommy got to the parking lot, he made a radio call to his office. When he finished, he walked over to Bob and said, "We need to talk. I need to pick your brain about what you know."

Bob replied, "I don't know shit. You know more than I do, and Gomez should know more than both of us. You need to pick his brain."

"No, I need to pick your brain. I want to know what JTF Six knows. I want to know what you learned about the smugglers back when you worked for your uncle up in the mountains twenty-odd years ago. We have to be proactive and stop this before it gets out of hand."

"Tommy, I really don't know much. What I do know is dated. If you want, I'll tell you what I learned when I was at Mountain Camp, but I gave you guys all that, the handheld photos, the aerial photos, and my observations. That's all old news."

"Bob, you know more. After Angelina was killed, you learned more. You learned so much that the whole bunch at Indian Springs up and left without a trace. Only serious dirt could do that. You had to have threatened to expose something really big. The only other answer would be that you killed them all, and I know that's not what happened. You're not Rambo. I just want to know what you know. It may be relevant to what is happening now."

Bob wasn't going to take this bait. He said, "Whatever I know from JTF Six is probably out of date and may still be classified. I'll talk to some folks and see if they'll brief you, but I don't hold out much faith in that. Everyone is trying to protect their own little empire. What I can do is keep an eye out for anything out of place in my country. As for information from twenty years ago, if I think of anything that I haven't shared with you, I'll let you know."

"OK, that's a start. Can you come with me to see the Sheriff?"

"Now?"

"Yes, he's in the office waiting for us."

Bob looked amused. "You're something, Tommy. OK, I'll follow you."

"Why don't you ride with me so we can talk. I'll give you a ride back here. I already told the Border Patrol folks your truck would be here for a while."

+++

When Bob got home in the evening, Diane had dinner ready. He'd called to let her know he'd be late. She knew there would be something to discuss after being tied up with the business of the dead girl for most of the day, so she waited.

They had always enjoyed dinner together. It was a good opportunity to talk things over. As they ate, Bob filled Diane in on the status of the young girl's murder investigation. He told her what Tommy had passed on to him. Essentially, they had nothing. She was a Jane Doe, probably from Mexico. She had never had a baby, and she was fifteen to eighteen years old. They had taken to calling her our Pollita rather than Jane Doe.

Diane said, "What about the baby?"

"They know nothing. The theory is that it is still with its mother, somewhere."

Diane was angry and said, "So, nobody cares? Is that right!"

Boby knew better than to argue this point. The truth was, there was nothing anyone could do. The mother and child were long gone. Hopefully doing OK. He lied, "The Border Patrol is looking for them."

Diane knew that was an attempt to calm her down. "Bull Shit," she said, "So what else did Tommy have for you? Telling you that would not have taken all afternoon."

"We met with the Border Patrol and the Sheriff."

Diane looked uneasy with this bit of news. "Why see them. What do they want from you?"

"Why do you think they want something from me?"

"I didn't just fall off the dog sled, or the turnip truck, as you like to say. I can understand you seeing Tommy about the dead girl, but the Border Patrol is not in the business of investigating murders, and the Sheriff's got better things to do, or so he thinks. One unidentified dead Mexican girl, or missing Mexican baby, isn't going to draw much attention from either of them."

Bob sat back, took a deep breath, and said, "They're worried about an increase in drug trafficking and illegals coming through here. They think maybe our Pollita got caught up in it somehow."

Diane gave Bob *the look* and said, "That doesn't answer my question."

"Boy, there's no putting one past you."

She smiled and punched him in the arm. "Let's hear it, old man."

Bob got serious and looked at this woman he'd been married to for the last twenty years. He could never hide anything from her. "They want me to tell them about before, about the Indian Springs days. They want to know what I learned while at JTF Six. The sheriff wants me to keep an eye on our country and the surrounding area."

She was not satisfied. "They can ask, but I know you're not telling them anything about what happened at Indian Springs over twenty years ago or your work at JTF Six. There's more. What else is there?"

"The sheriff wants to deputize me."

Diane looked at Bob with disbelief. "He can't do that. You're not a cop."

"The Arizona constitution says he can," Bob replied.

"No! I'm not having it. That's their job. You've done your part. You spent your life in service to your country. The kids and I shared you with the god damned army for years. How many weeks, months, years did we spend apart because you'd been sent off on some mission to God knows where? I'll tell you how many. Too many, that's how many. The kids may be grown and on their own now, but I'm still here. You're mine now. I'm not sharing you anymore."

Bob said nothing. Diane could see the sheepish look on his face. She threw her hands up in despair. "Wait, you already said yes!" It remained silent. "You did, didn't you?"

"Yes, but only as it affects the ranch. It gives me a little protection under the law."

Diane was mad. "What the hell does that mean, Bob? Are you only going to hunt for drug smugglers and coyotes on the ranch? The sheriff isn't going to pay you as a deputy to only keep an eye on our place."

"I'm not getting paid ..."

Before he could say more, Diane leaned forward and said, "You're not getting paid? That's even dumber than I thought. You're going to do their job and not even get paid? Damn Bob, start putting yourself and us first. You've earned it. We've earned it."

Diane leaned back in her chair. She couldn't stay mad at Bob for long, but she wanted to. She was deeply in love with this man. Their relationship began under trying circumstances when they were thrown together while escaping pursuit and striving to survive on the arctic tundra. To her surprise, their bond had lasted after they were safely away from the danger. It had even grown stronger over the course of more than twenty years of Army life.

Their relationship had survived frequently packing up the family and moving to postings around the world, sometimes with little notice. Often, she had dealt with extended periods of raising the kids on her own while Bob was in the Middle East, or Honduras, or some other god forsaken cesspool of humanity. Even more trying at times was the readjustment of having Bob back home after a year away. Surviving each challenge had made their bond stronger. Now they were settled into a quiet, stable life. She wanted no more drama. She wanted no more danger for her husband. She knew, however, that her wish for a quiet life was a chimera.

She said to herself, 'Suck it up, Diane.' You knew who you were marrying back then. She resigned herself to the reality of the situation. She would do whatever she could to help Bob and keep him safe. "OK, Bob, tell me everything. If I'm expected to support your decision, I need to know everything."

Bob explained what had been discussed: the worries about the south side of the border becoming more violent, the concern that there was going to be more drug smuggling coming across the remote sections of the border, and, most disturbing, a trend towards human smuggling on a larger scale.

The drug smuggling was high on everybody's radar, after all, the government had declared a war on drugs. In addition to federal assets being committed to the problem, lots of federal funds were being passed down to local law enforcement agencies. Border sheriffs and municipal police departments were more than willing to take advantage of that opportunity. If it meant participating in some counter-narcotic task forces, that was fine. The reward was worth it.

Bob said, "There are lots of assets being committed to the counter narcotics effort, which is fine with me. What bothers me is that there isn't much interest in the human smuggling problem. It's a sideshow."

Diane was a little perplexed, she said, "Bob, you've never had a problem with illegals crossing through the ranch. They're just people, honest people for the most part, trying to support their families back in Mexico. You leave water jugs and old clothes for them behind the spring house here and at Indian Springs camp. I've been at the pens when one or two Mexicans came out from hiding and approached you or your uncle. What did you do? You put them on for a day's wages, to help with the branding, or weaning, or spraying, or whatever job was going on that day. You didn't need the help. You did it to help them. Why do you care about this now? It makes no sense."

"It's not about a few folks trying to survive and better themselves. You know, I have no problem with that. The problem is it's changing. There are large groups being smuggled across the border. It's not the old contrabandistas or a few small-time coyotes that are doing it. It appears to be the drug cartels."

Diane said, "So, that's the Border Patrol's job, or Customs' job, or both their jobs for all I know. What I do know is it's not your job."

"I know."

"What are you going to do? Do you think you can stop it all on your own?"

"No, I can't stop it, but I can try and keep it off our place. I can keep us safe."

"Damnit, Bob, I don't like it. You be careful. After all we've been through, I'll be really mad if you get yourself killed."

With that, Bob stood up, walked over to Diane's end of the table, and kissed her on top of the head. "Remember the bear?"

Diane smiled and said, "Of course, I remember that smelly old bear." Years ago, the big brown bear had nearly killed them both, but they acted as a team; they stood their ground, and they lived. She remembered the surprise and unimaginable joy of realizing they were still alive as she pulled Bob out from under the big bear. "He never had a chance against us. We're a formidable team."

"Well," Bob said. "He was a lot tougher than these punks, and he was no match for us."

Diane got up from the table and said, "We were a lot younger then. If you'll do the dishes, I need to fold the laundry. Since you're bound and determined to get yourself killed, I think you should join me in the bedroom when you're done in the kitchen. I might not have many more chances to have my way with you." With that, she grabbed him by the butt and left the kitchen.

CHAPTER THREE

Tres Cruces Ranch, Cochise County, Arizona, October 1995

It was time for the fall works. One of the two times a year, every cowboy looked forward to. For cowboys, the spring works and fall works were the highlights of the year. Roping, branding, cutting, marking, and counting of calves took place during the spring works. That was when a rancher found out how he'd wintered over and what his calf crop was. The fall works was when all the work of the past year was rewarded. While doctoring, spraying, and branding of remnants missed in the spring works took place, the main focus was on the sorting of the cattle that were gathered. Bulls, replacement heifers, short-aged pairs, cull cows, and calves ready for market were sorted from the others. The replacement heifers were moved to a separate pasture until added to the herd of mother cows the next fall. Bulls were trailed to the bachelor pad for the winter. Weaned calves and cull cattle were shipped to the sale barn. While cowboys worked horseback most days, it was the works where their skills were tested, or more accurately shown off, while handling large numbers of cattle in a relatively short time.

When Tres Cruces acquired the Indian Springs Ranch in 1973, it added forty sections to the Tres Cruces one hundred twenty-six sections. Now the ranch totaled 166 sections. Each section, being a square mile of 640 acres, the operation now totaled 106,240 acres. Both ranches had their own infrastructure and were separated by the ridgeline running south to north along the top of the Chiricahua Mountains. With the barrier of the mountains between the ranches and only one forest service road crossing over the top between them, Jack had continued treating the two as separate ranches for the spring and fall works. Bob saw no reason to change that. He would start the Fall Works with the Indian Springs Camp, as the Indian Springs Ranch was now called. Today, Bob and Jim were driving over from headquarters, bringing a small string of three horses each.

Pat Ochoa and his wife, Suzie, would be following from Mountain Camp in an hour or so with Pat's horses. Suzie Solano, now Suzie Ochoa, and Bob went way back. They'd known each other since they were teenagers. Suzie had grown up at Mountain Camp, where her father, Cruz, had been the camp man for years. After nursing school, she married Pat Ochoa, a cowboy working for Jack Barnes. He'd put them at Mountain Camp, where they'd lived for the past twenty years, raising their family.

With the Indian Springs cattle already pushed off the mountains onto the flats by Malachi Snow, the camp man, a lot of the work was already done. Five cowboys should gather the three hundred fifty mother cows, their calves, and the bulls in three days, and push them into the two-section holding pasture with no problem.

On the fourth day, they would hold a rodeo, pronounced road ear, to separate the bulls and short-age pairs from the rest, then they'd push the cows and calves two miles to the pens. Bob had arranged for the stock truck to come at noon on day five. By then all the calves and cull cows should be sorted and ready to ship, the replacement heifers and any long ears that had been missed earlier would be trailered to a corral a few miles, and away branded if necessary and put on hay for a few days then turned out on the far east side of the ranch where the replacement heifers would stay for the next year. The freshly branded heifers and steers would spend a month with the replacement heifers until their brands peeled. Then it was off to the sale barn for them.

After everything was gathered, sorted, and shipped, it would be on to the fall works on the Tres Cruces side. With three times the number of cattle and over three times as much country, it would be a duplicate of what was done on the Indian Springs side, but on a larger scale. At least that was the plan.

Bob and Jim were taking the road over the mountains from Sabino Canyon to the San Bernardino Valley. As they came around a bend in the road near the top, Bob stopped. In front of him was a box truck blocking the road, or at least partially blocking the road. The front end was in a shallow ditch, with the cab doors open. There was nobody around. Bob and Jim got out of the ranch pickup. Bob told Jim to get the rifle out from behind the seat and cover him. Bob took his pistol from the holster on his chaps and started moving towards the truck. He stopped and listened. "Jim, do you hear that?"

"Yeah, I think it's coming from inside the truck."

Bob was thinking this was unusual; it had to be bad. No one would come over this mountain with a truck like this unless they were trying to hide something. "This is Foxtrot Uniform for sure; we need to be careful we're not walking into some bad shit. We need to clear the truck and our surroundings. You clear the passenger side. Be sure to check the ditch too. Let me know when you get to the back."

Soon Bob heard Jim say he was at the back of the truck. Bob told him to stay put while he cleared the driver's side. As soon as Bob had done that, he said, "Let's see what the hell's going on."

They could hear sounds from inside the cargo box. Somebody was knocking on the inside wall. Bob went to open the big sliding door. It was not only latched; it had been padlocked. "Jim, go get the post driver and caliche bar out of the pickup."

Jim was halfway to the truck by the time Bob finished. Good man, Bob thought. Then he slapped on the truck's door and shouted, "Can you hear me?" From inside, he could hear shouting in Spanish. It was muffled, and lots of different voices made it unintelligible. "Be quiet, be quiet," Bob said. He needed the people to relax. "Callense, por favor. Nosotros ser aqui a ayudar. We're here to help. Un momento mas."

Jim ran up with the post driver and caliche bar. Bob slid the post driver over the caliche bar, then climbed up on the bumper. He had Jim pass him the caliche bar and post driver. He positioned the chisel end of the caliche bar on the body of the padlock. "Jim, I need you to steady the bar on the lock. I'm going to raise the driver and then pound it down on the bar. That should spring the lock. Be ready to move your hands out of the way." With that, Bob drove the post driver onto the bar and sprung the lock.

In the second, it took Bob to toss the tools and jump down; Jim had already unlatched and started raising the door.

The smell greeted them even before the door was halfway open. It was the smell of human waste, sweat, and fear. The people inside were in a bad way. "Jim, go get the water can from the truck and some cups."

Soon, Jim was back with a five-gallon GI water can and a tube of paper cups that were destined for the Indian Springs round-up crew's meals. Bob helped the people out of the truck while Jim was busy handing out cups and pouring water for them. Bob started to check for injuries. There were a few deep cuts, some bumped heads, abrasions, some bruises, and at least two fractures. Nearly all of them were suffering from some degree of dehydration. Bob said under his breath, "They must have been in here for a while. Thank God it's not summer."

Bob told Jim to unload one of his horses and ride to Indian Springs Camp. He wanted the camp truck, some towing straps, and a heavy come-along. Some food and more water would be nice. Enough for a couple of dozen people. He also wanted bandages, antibiotic ointment, and a couple of air splints if there were any. Bob emphasized that the truck, water, and food were most important.

He would like the rest, but not if it took time to find. Jim was to call the Sheriff's office and the Border Patrol and fill them in on what was going on. Bob told him to say that Lieutenant Judson at the Sheriff's office should be notified. Soon, Jim was saddled up and ready to go. Bob said to him, "Don't kill that horse, but get there and back as quick as you can."

Once some order was established and all the people from the truck were seated on the ground, an older man came up to Bob and said, "My name is Juan. I speak English." Bob was relieved. He had all but used up his Spanish, which was mostly limited to cowboying and ordering food and beer.

Bob asked Juan, "What the hell is going on here?" Juan looked a little reticent to answer. "Look, Juan, the first thing is to get you help. Some of these people are in bad shape. I know you don't want La Migra involved, but what else can we do?"

Before this conversation could go any further, there was a distinct change in the voices of the group. Instead of the relatively quiet, even secretive tones of a moment ago, it was now louder, agitated, even indignant. Some of the group stood up, looking across the road. They pointed and waved their fists at a man coming out of the brush. They were yelling that he was a coyote. He was bloodied and appeared to have a hurt leg. He assumed a submissive posture and looked at Bob. Bob pulled his pistol and motioned the man forward.

Bob asked Juan, "Is this the driver of the truck?"

Juan said, "There were two men; he was not the driver; he was the guard."

"Was he armed?"

Juan said, "Yes, he had a rifle automático."

Bob held the young man at gunpoint, pulled a pigging string from his chaps, and tied him hand and foot. Some men from the truck came over and stared at the tied-up coyote with malice. They were grumbling, and Bob repeatedly heard coyote, pocho, cabrone, and chingadera flung in the direction of his prisoner. One of them spoke to Juan, looking at Bob.

Juan said, "They want you to look away."

"No, I can't allow that."

They were not happy with this and started to push past Bob towards the coyote. Bob held his arms out, stepping in front of the men, he said. "I am the deputy sheriff, Yo soy ayudante del sheriff. I say no. ¡Digo que no!" Then, pointing over to the group sitting on the ground, he waved them in that direction and said, "Sit down, please. Sientese, por favor."

"Thanks, man. Those pollos were going to kill me."

Bob looked at the young coyote. "Shut up, or I'll kill you."

"Come on, mister, don't be like that. You need to loosen the rope, it's too tight."

Bob looked disgusted with this young man. He was obviously a Chicano. He was Hispanic, but his English and accent said he was born or at least raised in the US. "If I need any shit out of you, I'll ask." The kid kept talking, so Bob went over to the stock trailer and pulled some old baling twine from the storage box. He twisted it, tied a large knot in the middle, and then gagged his prisoner.

While Bob was securing the gag, Suzie and Pat pulled up. Bob was relieved to see them. Suzie immediately took over caring for the injured. She sent Pat to their truck for her medical bag and instructed Bob on what he needed to do. She started an IV for an older woman who was doing poorly, splinted a couple of broken bones, and had seen to the minor injuries, all in an hour.

Bob, Pat, and Suzie were taking a break, waiting for the Sheriff and Border Patrol, when Suzie said, "Bob, you've been back for a year, and it seems like we're always busy. I've never had a chance to thank you properly for coming all the way back from Korea for Dad's funeral."

"It was the least I could do. He taught me how to cowboy. He taught me how to see and hear the land. Your father was a true friend. We don't get to have many of those in life." Bob smiled at Suzie and said, "Besides, he could sing with the coyotes."

Suzie laughed, "Yes, he could, and you're the only person from outside the family he ever showed that to."

She choked up a little and said, "It meant a lot to us and I'm sure to him," here she crossed herself, "that you were there for us and for him and at the funeral."

"You're welcome."

Suzie changed the subject and said, "After Angelina was killed, I was afraid you'd never find anyone else, but you did, and I'm glad. I really like her. She's not like anyone I've ever met before. Diane is a special person, but then she'd have to be to put up with you. You've done well."

Bob heard a vehicle approaching and stood up. As he reached his feet, he looked at Suzie and said, "I've been lucky twice."

It was Tommy Judson driving up. He parked and came over to the trio. "Good grief, Bob, what happened here?"

Bob said, "A couple of coyotes had those people locked in the back of that truck." Pointing to the tied-up coyote, he said, "He's one of them. It appears they ran off the road into the ditch, and hauled ass, leaving all their pollos locked in the back of the truck. Jim and I came on them about two hours ago. Suzie has patched them up, she said there are a few that need to go to the hospital."

Pointing at the young coyote, Tommy said, "He's one of the coyotes, you said. Where's the other?"

Bob indicated the group of illegals. They said this one was the guard and the other the driver. We never saw him. You'll need to talk to them to get better information. They told me they have been in the truck since the night before last."

Pointing at the coyote, Tommy asked, "Is he hurt?"

Yep, from the truck hitting the ditch, I think. He has a busted head and a bum leg, and he's no Mexican. He's Cholo."

About this time, Juan approached Bob and Tommy. There were two teenage girls with him. Juan looked uncomfortable. After some prodding from the girls, he said, "They want to tell you something." Juan looked very unsettled.

"What is it, Juan?" asked Bob.

"It is not right for me to say these things." Juan pointed at Suzie and said, "Better she help."

With that, Bob called to Suzie. "Suzie, can you come over here and translate for these two young women?"

Suzie came over and said, "Of course." She smiled at the girls and started to converse with them. As the conversation went along, it was obvious that Suzie was getting mad. The girls had loosened up and were chattering away excitedly. After a short time, Suzie held up her hand to quiet the girls and turned to Bob and Tommy.

"Something more than bringing illegals across the border is going on here. These two were recruited to work as waitresses in an expensive club in Hollywood, or so they were told. They're only fifteen and sixteen. They won't tell me where they're from, but I can tell you it's not from northern Mexico. Their accent is way different than most I hear. It's hard for me to understand some of it. Their idioms are unfamiliar. What I can understand is that they have been traveling for at least two weeks and getting raped on a regular basis, not by the other pollos but by the coyotes. Let me find out more. I'm going to see if Juan can help me. He's from down south, maybe he understands this accent better than I do."

Tommy said, "Good, find out what you can." Handing Suzie a notepad, Tommy asked, "Can you take notes?"

"Sure."

Then nodding towards the coyote, he said to Suzie. "Find out if he is one of the rapists."

"Ok," she said.

Tommy looked back at the two ranch trucks and stock trailers loaded with horses and said, "It looks like you had other plans today."

Bob shrugged, "I certainly never planned for this. We're starting the fall works today."

"I'm sorry to hold you up further, but I will need you to come to the office after the Border Patrol takes over here."

"No sweat, Tommy, this crew can do the job with or without me."

"Yeah, Bob, I'm sure, but this is a big deal for you ranchers. You have the right to be at least a little pissed."

Bob chuckled, "Remember what Uncle Jack told me over twenty years ago?"

"No, well maybe, something about they'll still be cows."

"Yeah, well, close enough." Bob looked at the illegals miserably awaiting their fate, at Suzie questioning the two teenage girls, and at the coyote acting smug. He said, "This is important. My crew can handle the fall works for a few days without me."

Just then, they heard a truck coming from the east. It was the Indian Springs pickup. Jim was driving as fast as the road would allow, kicking up quite a dust storm. Sitting next to him was the Indian Springs camp man, Malachi Snow, and his wife, Sariah. When they got out of the truck, the two men went straight to the back and unloaded a young man who had been hog-tied, blindfolded, and gagged. They dragged him up to Bob and Tommy. The illegals got excited and started yelling at him, as they had the other coyote earlier. "Here's the driver," said Jim with a smile, "and here's his pistol."

Jim explained how he had been moving downhill at a pretty good clip when the driver had stepped into the middle of the road, pulled his pistol on Jim, and demanded his horse. Jim never slowed down. He rode over him, knocking him to the ground, then hog-tied him and hurried to Indian Springs, where he told Malachi that Bob needed them in a hurry. They stopped on the way back and threw the driver into the truck bed.

While Jim was explaining all this, Sariah had brought tortillas, cookies, power bars, jerky, and Gator Aid from the truck and was handing it out to the illegals. Bob waved to get her attention and said, "Good job, Sariah." Then, addressing Jim and Malachi, Bob asked, "Did you bring the come-along and straps?"

"Yes, sir," answered Malachi.

Bob said, "Good, take a look at that truck and see if you can get it out of the ditch." Malachi Snow had the reputation of being a pretty fair mechanic and general innovator.

As Jim and Malachi were getting everything set up to pull the box truck out of the ditch, the Border Patrol pulled up from the west. There were four agents and two Suburbans. They came up to Tommy and Bob, looking over the scene.

Tommy said, "I'm glad to see you guys."

The senior Border Patrol agent said, "I bet you are. This looks like quite a haul. What can you tell me?"

Tommy and Bob filled them in on what they knew. The Border Patrol agent said he would send for more vehicles to get the pollos and coyotes to the detention center for processing and the hospital for the more seriously injured.

That was when Tommy said, "I'm keeping the coyotes and the two teenage girls. They are suspects and victims of felonies. I'm also keeping Juan to help interpret. The two males are under arrest and have been Mirandized. I intended to charge them with rape, kidnapping, unlawful imprisonment, assault with a deadly weapon, and whatever else I can come up with. I think they're Americans, so they're mine anyway.

The two females are the victims of repeated rape by these two. I need to get detailed statements from them. I'm keeping them for a while. I'll keep you posted on their status. I need Juan because it seems they're from the Yucatan, and their Spanish is laced with a lot of unfamiliar idioms and vocabulary. Juan understands them pretty well."

The senior Border Patrol didn't like this idea, and he let it be known.

Tommy said, "Why don't you contact Agent in Charge Gomez. I'm sure he'll be OK with this."

+++

The Border Patrol had arranged to have the box truck towed to their station. Bob's crew had made it over the mountain and were getting everything ready to start the works in the morning. Bob and Tommy had stopped at the Tres Cruces headquarters to let Diane know what was going on.

When Bob and Tommy had stopped at the ranch headquarters to notify Diane of the change in plans and what had happened with the illegals, she had insisted that she drive Bob to the Sheriff's office and be included in any discussions. "I may not have anything to add about what you found today, but I have a right to know about everything that happens on our ranch." Tommy had tried to protest Diane's presence but gave it up as a bad idea when he jokingly referred to the fact that Bob had been deputized. She said. "That, mister deputy sheriff, is not a place you want to go."

Bob shot Tommy a warning look. Tommy was wise enough to let it drop with a quiet, "Sorry."

An hour later, Tommy, Bob, and Diane were settling into a conference room at the sheriff's office. Tommy had provided each with a notepad and offered coffee or tea. Both Diane and Bob accepted the offer for tea. The discussion centered around Tommy getting all the information he could from Bob about the day's events. When he figured he had all the details. He said, "Bob, I'll have this typed up for you and ready to sign tomorrow. Can you call me in the morning to set up a time?

"Sure, I'll give you a call."

The meeting broke up, and Diane excused herself and headed for the ladies' room. Once she was out of earshot, Tommy said, "I need to apologize for getting Diane mad."

Bob answered, "Not to me, you don't."

Tommy looked a little uneasy. "I'm not sure I want to bring it up again. That's a tough woman."

Bob smiled and said, "One day, when we're both old and gray, and drawing social security, I'll tell you the story about how we met, and maybe her past. You have no idea of how strong she really is."

"Why not now?"

"Nice try, but no, you have to wait. I will say my wife is the toughest person I know, but also the most loyal and the warmest I know. Get on her good side and you have an ally forever."

Tommy said, "I guess if you get on her bad side, you have an enemy forever."

"No, she has no time to waste on the assholes of the world unless they pose a danger to her or hers."

"That sounds like a good philosophy," said Tommy.

"Yep, it works for her."

Tommy asked, "And you, does it work for you?"

Bob smiled and answered. "I'm a work in progress."

When Diane returned from the restroom, she and Bob decided to stop at a little Mexican restaurant for dinner on their way home. It sat on the road between Bisbee and Naco. It didn't look like much, just some tables with plastic tablecloths, plastic chairs, and all the ambiance of a gas station. It had, in fact, been a convenience store not long ago. The food, unlike the atmosphere, was excellent.

Once they were finished with dinner and were walking across the parking lot towards the truck, Diane stopped, took Bob's arm, and, looking to the west, she said, "Look, it's God's paintbrush." The mammatus clouds, made up of descending bumps that resembled human breasts, were blazing blood red, fading to gold on the horizon over the Huachuca Mountains.

"It never gets old," said Bob.

CHAPTER FOUR

Bisbee, Arizona, October 1995

Bob was sitting at the conference table at the Sheriff's office, waiting for Tommy to bring him his statement to sign. As he sat there thinking of a lot of nothing, the Sheriff walked in. "How are you, Bob?"

Bob stood, shook the Sheriff's hand, and answered, "I'm doing fine, and you?"

"Oh, you know, the normal stuff that rural law enforcement deals with, most things are about the same, except for this increase in illicit cross-border traffic. So far, the two incidents over at your place are the worst, but what's even more unsettling is so many reports from across the county about evidence of large groups of illegals. Lots of remote water points are being trashed with empty water jugs, abandoned backpacks, and clothing. There is also evidence of increased vehicle activity at these same water points, along pipeline roads, railroad right of ways, and washes. Border Patrol apprehensions are climbing to unprecedented highs for this area. There are lots of illegals moving through here, and I'm afraid lots of drugs are being smuggled through here as well."

Bob said, "Well, it sounds like you've got your hands full."

"Yeah, we are getting busier with this stuff, but we're keeping it together. Mr. Hasett, there is going to be a meeting next month at Fort Huachuca. It is to discuss cooperation between the different agencies. We need to come up with an approach for working together. I would like you to attend as the voice of the local ranchers."

Bob replied, "I don't know what I can add, but if it helps, I'll be there."

Just then, Tommy came into the room. "Sheriff, do you have a minute for an update on this?" he said, holding up the statement. "Yes, come to my office." The Sheriff thanked Bob for his time and excused himself.

As the Sheriff left the room, Tommy said to Bob, "Here it is." Handing Bob the typed statement. "Read it over, make any needed changes, and initial them. I'll be back in a few minutes." With that, Tommy left to see the Sheriff.

Later, Tommy walked Bob out to his truck in the parking lot. "How about joining me for a bite?" Tommy asked.

"Sure, where did you have in mind?"

"I have to go to Douglas, how about the Sonic?"

"Sure, that works for me." Answered Bob.

+++

After getting their meals, Bob and Tommy parked away from the drive-in a little. They were standing at the back of Bob's truck, using the tailgate as a table. Tommy said, "We questioned the two coyotes you caught about our dead Pollita. They denied any involvement, but they weren't convincing. I can't say they are directly involved, but I think they know, or think they know who is. We're keeping pressure on them to see what they give us. We think they're part of a new gang that has moved into Tucson."

"What's the name of the gang?" asked Bob.

"They keep feeding us conflicting answers. One time it's MS13, the next time it's Del Norte, but my favorite is KAC for Crazy Ass Chicanos. I don't think it's any of these."

Bob chuckled, "KAC for Crazy Ass Chicanos? It seems spelling is not their strong suit. Is there a link between them and Pollita?" Bob had started dropping the, our, from the dead girl's moniker.

"They won't say yet. They're holding back, looking for a deal. We want a lot more out of them. Since we have them on a bunch of felony charges, and they're starting to squirm. We're being patient. There are a couple of things in our favor. They're not as smart, experienced, or tough as they pretend to be. They haven't lawyered up yet, and I think they may be afraid of getting in the system with some genuinely bad guys."

Bob thought about all this and asked, "Is it possible they were poaching on somebody else's territory?"

"I think so. They slipped once and mentioned not paying the tax."

Bob looked interested in this turn of phrase. "Tax, like a toll for crossing someone's property?"

"Yep, that's what I think. There is a tax precedent with drug smugglers."

Bob said, "Can you confirm that the drug cartels are now smuggling people?"

Tommy answered, "No, we can't. It might be the drug cartels, or it might be copycats using a proven method. After we finish lunch, I'm going back to continue interrogating them."

"Do you think you can get anything out of them?" Bob asked.

"I think so, after a night in jail with some serious gang bangers, they're pretty scarred. I'm going to press the point that they violated the tax rule; that's the kind of stuff that gets errant drug smugglers killed. I'm assuming the same rules apply to anyone crossing a cartel's country. You know, like people smugglers, as well as drug smugglers. If that got out, it would be the end of them. If we threatened to release it to the press, it should push them to cooperate."

"Sounds pretty harsh."

Tommy gave Bob an incredulous look and responded with some pique. "Coming from you, that's the epitome of irony. You know that, don't you?"

"Yeah, but I'm not one of the saints, or a holder of the priesthood, you are."

"Don't try to shame me, Bob Hasett. We've both walked a bit too close to the edge." Then, looking at Bob with a touch of certitude, "Or maybe one of us even leapt right off into the depths of depravity. I can say I never betrayed my faith or failed justice. Can you?"

Bob was surprised by Tommy's irritation. "Tommy, I'm sorry if I got under your skin. It wasn't my intention. I'm the last person to judge your character. I know you as a god-fearing man of strong faith and sound morals. If you say what you're doing is consistent with your standards, I believe you." Bob thought hard about what he was about to say. "I never did anything that didn't feel just or necessary at the time. I always believed my actions were vindicated as the right response to evil. When I look back, I can say I wouldn't change anything I did. I was dealt some hard cards, and I played a hard hand. Just be careful, you can't run from your conscience."

"I'm aware of that. My conscience is suffering no pangs of guilt." Tommy gathered up his trash and started for his truck. "I need to get back to the office. I'll keep you posted."

Bob was thinking about how confusing people could be. He sighed and said, "See you, Tommy."

+++

The fall works were going well. All the Indian Springs cattle were gathered, sorted, and shipped. The Tres Cruces work was well over halfway done. Bob was enjoying a bit of relaxation at the wagon camp, sitting on a camp chair by the cookfire. He had changed from his brown Carhartt brush jacket to a little warmer blanket-lined Walls coat. His wild rag, a sky-blue square yard of silk, was double wrapped around his neck and tied with a square knot in front. He had his hat pulled down tight. He was holding a hot cup of tea between his hands. His round-up crew of four cowboys was gathered on the far side of the fire. The sun had set, the sky was clear, the stars were bright, and it was cold. Not like the cold in Alaska or Korea, but it was near freezing. There would be plenty of frost on the ground by morning. Diane pulled a chair up and sat beside him.

"I appreciate your coming out to bring Cookie's supplies. How about staying the night and sharing my bedroll?"

She grinned, "No. I have to get back tonight."

"Why not? You kept me from freezing in Alaska. I may need that tonight."

Diane laughed, "Yeah, and look where that got us."

Bob squeezed her arm and said, "Look around, I wouldn't change a thing."

Diane hooked her arm under Bob's and said, "So, three or four days before you're all back at headquarters?"

"Yep, it's all going pretty well. Would you call Leon tomorrow and be sure we've still got trucks set up for the twenty-third?"

"Of course."

"Tell him I expect to ship around six hundred twenty-five yearlings and one hundred cull cows. The yearlings should average about four hundred fifty pounds."

"Where do you want them to go, Willcox?"

"Ask Leon what he thinks. He usually has his ear to the ground."

"OK," she said, "Well, I'd better go."

"How's Aunt Maria doing?"

"She claims she's fine, but she's not. She's missing Uncle Jack really bad, and she thinks she's a burden to us. She keeps talking about going to the Pioneer's Home or getting an apartment in town. It's sad, such a strong woman reduced to feeling alone and useless."

"What can we do?"

Diane had been thinking about this for a few days. "You're going to be working out of headquarters for a few days."

"Yep, we'll spend the last five or six days working from there," answered Bob.

"I think you should ask Maria to cook breakfast for the crew while you're there. That will give Cookie a little break, and Maria will be helping. She needs to feel useful."

"That sounds like a plan. You tell Aunt Maria, and I'll let Cookie know."

"Will he be OK with that?"

"Let's see, a break from getting up at three thirty in the morning and going to bed at nine o'clock in the evening, yeah, I think he'll be fine with that as long as his pay isn't cut."

Diane stood up to go. "Good, she'll enjoy being useful."

Bob stood up and walked Diane to the Bronco, gave her a kiss, and said, "See you in a few days."

She looked up at the stars and said, "I remember crisp nights, gazing at the night sky with a young man. Were the stars just as bright there?"

"I think they were, and the northern lights were spectacular," Bob answered.

"Yes, they were." She paused for a moment, then asked, "Bob, do you ever miss it?"

"Sometimes, but I like this too, besides," he said, pointing to his head, "I have it in here."

Diane gave him a squeeze on the butt and said, "We still do pretty well, old man." She then got into the Bronco and left.

+++

It was cold. Bob was burrowed deep within his bedroll. César Robles, commonly called Cookie, had just awakened him and was now walking through camp to wake up John Tessay, the youngest cowboy in the crew. Being the youngest and newest meant he was the jingle boy. It was his job to find and gather the horses for the day's work.

Everyone else was asleep and would stay that way for another hour or so until breakfast was ready, and the horses were in. Bob didn't want to get up; it was warm in his bedroll, and it would be cold once he crawled out from under the blankets, but he was the boss. With the exception of Cookie, he made a point of being the first up and last to bed.

Bob wandered over to the fire and poured himself a cup of hot coffee. Robles returned from waking the jingle boy and said, "Morning, Jefe."

Bob saluted him with the cup of coffee, "Morning, Cookie."

"How's the coffee?"

"Perfect, hot, black, and strong but not burnt. You must have found a clean sock to boil the grounds in."

Cookie grunted, "Maybe not so clean."

Bob explained about Maria Barnes handling the breakfasts when they returned to headquarters for the last few days of the works. Cookie surprised Bob by readily agreeing to the idea.

Bob said, "I thought you might not be in favor of someone else cutting into your bailiwick and cooking in your kitchen."

Cookie thought about this for a minute. "If it was someone else, I might not like it, but I've been the wagon cook here for better than ten years. Jack and Maria were always good to me. If Doña Maria wants to cook in my kitchen, Dios mio, she is welcome to. I'll even do the dishes for her."

"Thanks, Cookie."

"No problem, Jefe."

"What's for breakfast?"

Cookie smiled, "Different from yesterday. Today it's Huevos a la Mexicana, beans, chorizo, and tortillas."

"Outstanding, Cookie, keep up the good work."

"Jefe, you know La Senora's breakfasts are much hotter than mine. She really likes the chilies. When these gringos of yours start eating her breakfast, you're going to hear them calling from the baño for todos los santos."

Bob smiled, "Can't wait."

The cowboys were lining up for breakfast as Bob finished his. After he scraped his plate and put it and his flatware in the tub of hot, soapy water, he heard the unmistakable high-pitched, short hoop of John bringing in the remuda.

Bob went over to the bin with the oats and put half a coffee can of oats into a morral. While the cowboys were eating their breakfast, he went to the corral, caught his horse for the day. Boxer was a big, bald-faced chestnut of better than sixteen hands and as wide as a tanker truck. Bob liked this horse. He was strong, fast, and cow smart. If there was any complaint about Boxer, it was that his idea of a trot was more like beating the ground into submission. Bob hobbled Boxer's front feet, put the feed bag on him, brushed off the worst of the dirt, and saddled him.

When Bob finished his morning routine of brushing his teeth, shaving, and knocking down a final cup of coffee, he went back to the corral, shook out a loop in his rope, and prepared for the daily ritual of catching horses for the crew. The cowboys had finished breakfast and joined Bob at the corral. He would call the name of a cowboy, and the cowboy would call out the name of his horse for the day. Each had a string of seven horses for the works. Bob would then toss a houlihan loop over the horse's head, catching him for the cowboy. This was repeated for each cowboy.

While the cowboys were getting their horses ready, Gabe came over to Bob. "I always enjoy this part of the day, even if you don't really need to rope these ponies."

Bob answered, "Yeah, you could walk up to most of them with a morral and be done with it." Bob looked at Gabe, an old buckaroo who came down every year from Nevada, or Idaho, or whatever big outfit in the Great Basin he was working for at the time, to help with the spring and fall works. He was an old friend of Jack Barnes. Bob smiled at him and said, "Tradition, Gabe, it's important, especially for the young ones. They like it, it makes them feel punchy."

Gabe laughed, "I've punched cows all over the western half of the United States." He waved his arm in a broad arc, indicating the surrounding landscape. "This country will make a cowboy of anybody that'll let it. This crew is plenty punchy."

Bob saw that everyone was ready. "I know, maybe it's me that likes it." With that, he shoved his foot in the stirrup and swung up. Keeping with range etiquette, the rest of the crew immediately followed except for Jim Cooper. He had the rough string and today's mount, Mouse, was green and known to be humpy on a cold morning, or even a bit bronco. The other cowboys sat their horses in a circle around Jim as he mounted. If his horse decided to make a rodeo out of it, the others would ride in and crowd him. When Jim mounted, there was no show this morning, at least not until they were about a hundred yards out, when Mouse decided to test Jim. Mouse lost.

Amidst the congratulatory whooping and hollering of the cowboys who always enjoyed a good bronc ride, Bob called to Jim, "Don't be afraid to ride the attitude out of that pinche grulla. Twenty years ago, I had his great uncle in my string. His name was Nobody, and he was a knucklehead, but there was no finding his bottom. Keep him under you, and it'll be a good day."

It was mid-morning. Bob had thrown his circle, putting Gabe on the far east side and himself on the far west side with the other three cowboys spaced in between at half-mile intervals. They were gathering the cattle and pushing them south to the cross fence that separated Dart Pasture from West Pasture. The fact that it was open with no big mesquite bosques or many deep washes should make it an easy day.

Ahead of Bob were several dust clouds. Some were pretty small, and some were quite large. Each cloud marked the progress of a group of bovine critters moving along at a steady pace, kicking up the dust as they shuffled along on various cow trails. Bob was happy. The dust clouds were all moving south and drifting to the west, in the right direction to put the cattle at the corner gate to West Pasture. These girls had been doing this every fall for as long as they'd been alive. They knew the drill. So far, everything was going pretty well. There had been no jackpots of either the minor or major kind. As far as he could tell, no one had broken the circle, nor was anyone afoot.

Before long, Bob was following about a hundred head that were lined out, swinging along on the trail next to the western boundary fence. He was completely relaxed and talking to his horse. He said, "Life is good." Then it wasn't.

A mile or so up ahead, a large dust cloud was too far to the west. It was not a vehicle on the road; it was too big and moving too slow. It had to be cows. Bob put his horse up into a gallop, swinging wide to the east to avoid spooking or stopping the cattle he'd been trailing. He needed to get to what he suspected was a downed fence and plug the hole.

When he had covered the distance, he found that indeed it was a downed fence. It wasn't just a broken wire or two. All four wires had been cut and folded back. This was intentional. He couldn't see any tire tracks. If there were any, the cows had walked all over them. His first task was to stop any more cows from going through the hole. As he sat his horse in the middle of the gap in the fence, he started to put together a plan to address the problem. He had temporarily fixed the first problem of plugging the hole, but much more needed to be done.

Soon, he saw the unmistakable dust cloud of a lone horseman moving towards him at a fast clip. It was Pat Ochoa, the cowboy next to Bob in the circle. He stopped on the other side of the trailing cattle that were still filing to the south past Bob and the downed fence. "What can I do, Boss?"

"That depends. What's it look like out there?" Said Bob, pointing to the south and east.

"It's odd. Everything was going fine, but now it looks like the cows out ahead are bunching up and some are turning back."

With that, Bob walked his horse back through the fence, stepped down, and pulled out his fencing pliers. "Come give me a hand with this."

Motioning towards the cattle, Pat asked, "What about these girls?"

"They're fine for now. If need be, we'll worry about them tomorrow. I'm more concerned about what's wrong up ahead." The cows that had gotten through the downed fence were walking down the road towards the south. Bob motioned to the cows that were moving down the road, "As for those, they're headed in the right direction. We'll deal with them after we see what's wrong."

Once Bob and Pat had patched the fence, they set out to the southeast towards what looked like something of a cow wreck. The dust cloud was rising and not moving in any particular direction. A sign that the cattle were milling about. One cowboy was hooping and working hard to keep the cows moving to the south. Bob rode up to him and asked what the problem was. The cowboy, John Tessay, said, "Something up ahead has got them spooked."

"Back off a little, they'll find their way around whatever it is. I'm going to see what's wrong up ahead. By the way, we sprung a leak onto the road. Don't worry about that. Pat and I will deal with them." Pointing towards the road, Bob said, "There's a fair-sized bunch moving south along the fence. Hopefully, they'll keep going to the gate. Keep an eye out for them. I'll see you guys at camp. Let Gabe and John know."

As Bob and Pat rode to the south, they passed cattle that were milling around or stopped, or, in some cases, turning back to the north. Bob told Pat to leave them be. He wanted to know what was causing the problem.

They were approaching a water lot called Adobe Tank that seemed to be the obstacle to the cattle's movement south. Adobe Tank was a steel holding tank filled by Adobe Springs via a two-mile-long pipeline. It had two drinkers and a small wire corral around it.

Once there had been an adobe shed, but now all that was left was the foundation with a weather, melted mud brick wall of maybe two feet in height. Like most water points in the area, it had a small grove of cottonwood and mesquite trees that were watered by the overflow from the storage tank.

When they were a couple of hundred yards away, Bob reined in his horse and pulled his pistol. There, hanging from the lower limb of a cottonwood tree, was a dead beef. He saw two men working on it. They were busy dressing the animal and didn't see him.

Bob motioned for Pat to come up beside him. He pointed to the men at Adobe Tank. "You're not armed, but they don't know that. If you're game, I want you to stay close behind me, a little to the left. I'm going to confront them."

"I'm game," answered Pat.

With that, Bob kicked Boxer into a gallop, and in a few seconds, he'd closed the distance to the men at Adobe Tank. Sliding his horse to a stop, he drew down on the two men and hollered, "Hands up, manos arriba!"

One of the men broke for a rifle leaning against the trunk of the cottonwood. He didn't make it. Bob quickly dropped him a few feet from his goal.

He then rode past the downed man and grabbed the rifle leaning against the cottonwood. It was a lever-action thirty-thirty carbine, with a full tube magazine of six rounds and a round in the chamber. The other man had tried to run, but Pat had roped him and jerked him down before he covered twenty feet.

Bob stepped down and checked the man he'd shot. The bullet had hit him high in the thigh, breaking his femur. Blood was pumping out in spurts. Bob removed the man's belt, making it into a tourniquet. Amid the wounded man's loud and tearful protests, Bob tied the tourniquet tight over a short stick, then twisted the stick until the worst of the arterial bleeding stopped. He finished securing the stick, then dragged the wounded man to the cottonwood and sat him against the trunk. Just then, John Tessay rode up. "I heard a shot."

Bob pointed at the wounded man. "Yep, we're OK. That one went for his rifle, the other tried to run, but Pat used him for roping practice."

Tessay looked at the beef hanging from the tree limb. "Looks like you found the problem."

"Yep. John, I need you to get word to the Sheriff. Do you know where the Slim Jenkin's cow camp is on the road at the base of that hill?" Bob pointed towards a cone-shaped hill a few miles to the southwest.

"Yes, if it's the one with the old trailer, adobe barn, and windmill tower with no windmill."

"That's it. We need a deputy and an ambulance. Tell them to come to Adobe Tank. If they don't know where that is, tell them you'll meet them at the Long Tom Canyon gate. If no one is at the camp, use your imagination, but don't break in. Slim's a pretty unforgiving type."

John nodded his understanding and left at a lope.

Bob was questioning the two men. He knew that the authorities would prefer he not do it, but he needed to know what was going on. What he gleaned from them was that they were not local. He suspected they were from Sanora or Sinaloa.

They were wearing the expensive, overlong, pointed-toe boots with silver toe caps, tight jeans, tight-fitting snap button shirts with silver collar tabs, and black straw hats that were almost a uniform for the younger Mexican gang thugs. These were not peons or campesinos trying to find work. These were young toughs in the business of smuggling drugs or people.

Suddenly, John Tessay was galloping at full speed back towards them. Behind him was a dust trail. A lone vehicle was chasing him on the dirt track that led to Adobe Tank. Bob and Pat heard gunshots. John swung over the side of his horse with only his right leg over the saddle. Holding the horn in his right hand, he had the horse between him and the vehicle. As he approached the water lot, he slid his horse to a stop, leapt off, and said, "Those assholes are trying to kill me."

Bob had already taken up the rifle and handed Pat his pistol, telling him to keep an eye on their prisoners. Pat told Tessay to take the horses behind the storage tank. Bob was already in a firing position with some concealment and good cover behind the old adobe wall. The vehicle, a pickup with a camper shell, was closing fast, way too fast for the condition of the dirt track. The truck slid to a stop in a cloud of dust. A man jumped out of the passenger door with an AK-47 rifle at his hip, pointed in Bob's general direction, and started shooting. He was using the spray and pray method of firing as many indiscriminate shots as he could, as fast as he could. Bob did not rush; he squeezed the trigger. The gunman dropped. Another man was exiting the driver's side at the same time. He dropped to the ground and started calling out, "Don't shoot, don't shoot."

Bob did not answer. He was not going to give away his position.

The driver continued, "Please listen, you've made a big mistake. You have no idea who you're dealing with." Bob kept quiet. Eventually, the driver of the truck would make a mistake. "We can work this out. Let me talk to you. You don't want this kind of trouble. Let's talk before this gets worse for you. I can talk to my boss. I can make it alright for you. Let's talk."

Bob was entertained by this. He was under no illusions about working anything out. The driver continued to try and make his point. Bob decided it was time to act. "Stand."

"What?"

Bob waited. Finally, the man stood up.

Bob said, "Walk forward."

"What? I can't hear you."

Bob was not familiar with this rifle, so he wasn't sure just how close he could miss. He knew he could hit center mass at this short range, but a shot between the feet might hit meat and not dirt. Bob looked at the driver beside the truck and saw the butt of the pistol in his waistband. Bang! Dirt kicked up between the driver's feet, a little closer to the right foot than he intended. "Note to self," Bob said under his breath, "zero is right of center."

"Holly Shit, cabrón! You nearly blew my foot off." Bang! Even closer to the right foot. "OK, OK, pendejo. I'm walking, I'm walking," said the driver.

"Toss the pistol." He did.

Bob let him come to within a few feet of the adobe wall, then stood up from behind cover. "Pat, John, come out."

"Keep them covered. I need to check out the truck," said Bob.

Looking at the man with the wounded leg, John said, "He'll die if we don't get him help. I can leave now."

"Lucky for him, I know how to put on a tight tourniquet. He may lose his leg, but he's not going to die any time soon from that wound, and that's his good fortune."

John was a little confused and uncomfortable with the Boss's casual attitude. "Good fortune, how is that his good fortune?"

Bob was walking towards the truck when he said, "It's his good fortune that I haven't already killed him."

John raised his eyebrows, and he shot Pat an enquiring look. Being new to the Tres Cruces crew, John Tessay didn't know how to take the boss. Pat, on the other hand, had been working and living on the ranch for two decades. He had known Bob all that time. Pat gave John a reassuring look. "Don't worry about Bob. He knows what he's doing."

As Bob approached the truck, he saw that the man who had sprung out of the passenger's door appeared to be dead. There was a large exit wound between his shoulder blades. Bob thought, right through the spine, which explains why he dropped like a sack of potatoes. Bob prodded him roughly with his foot. When there was no reaction, he touched the muzzle of the rifle against the shooter's eyeball. Nothing. Bob rolled him over and saw the hole just below his sternum. He was lying dead in a pool of blood that was soaking into the dirt. Bob collected the shooter's Kalashnikov rifle, went through his pockets, and checked out the truck. The cab and camper were empty except for some weed that Bob had left alone and a couple of thirty-round magazines for the AK-47, which he had collected.

Walking back to the water lot, Bob considered his situation. He was not one bit happy with it. These people, these cartel thugs, or gangbangers, or whatever they were called, were all the same. They had no scruples; they had no sense of morality; they were soulless; they were the epitome of evil. They had some perverse sense of honor that was in no way honorable. It was, in fact, abhorrent to anything decent or honorable. The only thing these people understood was force.

Now he'd had a shootout with them. They'd want revenge. They were in no way adverse to taking it out on his family, his ranch, and his crew, including their families. He felt a hard lump in his stomach.

The only thing that made sense was to finish off these scum bags. As much as he knew it was the only way to guarantee the safety of his family and crew, he knew he wasn't going to kill them in cold blood. He said to himself, "You're getting soft, old man. They should already be worm food. Maybe they'll do something stupid and give you an excuse to end this now."

The driver of the pickup asked, "Is he going to make it?"

Bob said nothing.

The driver looked distressed. "Is he dead?"

Bob said sarcastically, "Why, you feeling lonely? Want to join his dead ass?" Bob may not be willing to kill this thug in cold blood, but he was not averse to prodding him into a foolish act.

The driver started towards Bob. "Chinga a tu puta madre! He's my brother."

Holding the rifle with his left hand on the fore end hand guard and his right hand grasping the waist of the butt stock just behind the trigger guard, he stepped forward with his right leg while swinging the rifle butt from his waist in a vertical stroke that smashed up into the driver's chin, snapping his head back and causing his knees to buckle as he stumbled backwards.

Bob was now sideways to the driver with his right side towards his advisory. The rifle was parallel to the ground, just above his shoulder, with the butt towards Bob's front. He took a long stride with his right foot towards the driver, ramming the butt of the rifle into his face. The driver went down. Bob said, "He was your brother."

John asked with a note of disapproval, "Do you think that helped?"

"It helped me. Is that a problem for you?"

"No, sir."

Bob was seething with anger. His family and everyone on the ranch were now in danger due to these men. He wanted them to do something stupid. He wanted an excuse to end this now and be done with it. He went over to Pat, who knew exactly what the deal was. "Pat, I can insult that cholo all day, but my

Spanish isn't good enough to get the other two pissed enough to attack. How about you do it?"

"Sure, what's the plan? Get them to attack, kill them, and dispose of the bodies?"

"Yep,"

Pat asked, "Why bother with getting them to attack. Why not just kill them?"

"John'll never go along with it. I'm not sure he'll go along with it either way. He might insist on notifying the sheriff even if we can claim self-defense."

Pat was as unhappy about the situation as Bob was. "Yep, I think he would."

Pat walked over to John and slapped him. John reeled back and started to respond when Bob shouted for him to stop. Pat then said to John, "You know that because you're here, we're going to have to turn these pendejos over to the sheriff."

"So, that's what we're supposed to do."

"What, I thought you were some kind of bad ass Apache. I thought you'd get it. Well, I guess not, so here's the deal. We shouldn't turn them over to the Sheriff. We should stuff their dead asses in a rat hole where they'd never be found, but no, not now, now we're going to tell the sheriff because of your pussy ass." Pointing to their prisoners, he continued, "These maricones are going to tell their bosses what happened. That puts me, my wife, and kids, and everyone else on this ranch in danger."

"No, that can't be."

Pat was so mad that he was trembling. "Yes, it can be. It's easy for you to say stupid shit like that. In a couple of weeks, your ass'll be back on the reservation, hundreds of miles from here, safe and snug. We'll be here looking over our shoulders."

"OK, maybe you're right." John looked at Bob and said, "You can trust me, I won't say anything."

With that, Pat handed him the pistol and said, "Shoot them."

John was completely taken aback by this. He'd done plenty of hunting on the reservation in the White Mountains. He knew how to handle firearms, and he was not squeamish, but this made no sense. "No." He handed the pistol back to Pat.

Bob was not surprised. As much as he wanted this problem to go away, he was somewhat relieved. "OK, no one's killing anybody. Let's get them tied up."

Bob pulled a pigging string from his chaps, rolled the groggy driver onto his stomach, and told Pat and John to secure the other two. He tied the driver's ankles, then, pulling them nearly to his waist, he bent the driver's arms behind his back and tied his wrists to his ankles. "That should hold him." He then went through the driver's pockets and found an Arizona driver's license with a Phoenix address, quite a lot of cash, and some other odds and ends. Bob stood holding the driver's license of the driver and his dead brother. He noted they for both was Phoenix.

The two cowboys had finished their task and were standing, waiting. Bob said, "Pat, I want you to go get those cows off the road like we started to do. John, go with him. I expect the cattle will be near Slim Jenkins' camp by the time you get there. John, give the sheriff's office a call. Ask for Tommy Judson and fill him in. If he's not in, pass the information to whoever is available. Tell them we have one dead, one gunshot wound and one concussion, and one unharmed. At least two are Mexican nationals; the other two appear to be American. Repeat the message to me."

John repeated what Bob wanted him to pass on to the Sheriff's office. Bob listened and then added, "Don't forget to offer to meet them at Long Tom Canyon gate."

John said, "OK, but we can't both go and leave you here alone with these guys."

"Why are you worried about them not being alive when you get back?"

John looked a little flustered. "Why, no. What if they jump you?"

"Then I'll kill them."

"But, there are three of them…"

Pat interrupted John's protest. "Let's go, junior. The Boss will be fine." Nodding towards the three prisoners, he continued, "No hill for a climber, right, Boss?"

"Right, Cherries, the lot of 'em." Bob continued, "Pat, if the deputies don't need John to guide them, he can help you with the cows. Is that all clear?"

Both answered, "Yes, boss." With that, the two cowboys swung up on their horses and started off at a trot.

CHAPTER FIVE

Headquarters Tres Cruces Ranch
Cochise County, Arizona, October 1995

Bob was horseback in the sorting alley. A cowboy would push a bunch of cows and calves into the alley, then Bob would ease forward and cut off one, two, or sometimes three, push them to the other end of the alley, and call out, Ship, Keep, or Through. The three cowboys on the gates at the end of the alley would then know which gate to open. This way the shipper steers, heifers, and cull cows were in one pen, the replacement heifers and slick or undersized calves were in another pen, and the mother cows were in the main corral.

Halfway through the sorting, Tommy Judson drove up. He spoke to Diane, who was keeping a tally on the sorting. After a while, she motioned to Bob that he was needed. He called over, saying that as soon as he finished with the bunch that was in the alley, he would take a break. A few minutes more was all he needed.

When the alley was cleared, he told the cowboys to take a short break and rode over to where Tommy and Diane were standing on the scale's catwalk. Whatever brought Tommy out here instead of making a phone call must be important. Bob stepped down from Crescent, his top horse, and walked up to Tommy. "Howdy Tommy, what brings you here?"

Tommy looked around uneasy; there were too many people around. "Not here."

"OK, Diane, please take Tommy to the house while I get the crew lined out, if you could ask Aunt Maria to take over the tally book. I'll join you soon."

When Bob entered the house, Tommy was drinking some lemonade, and Diane was talking to Aunt Maria. Diane had handed the tally book to Maria, who was going out to the corral to fill in for Diane. Maria had a smile on her face. Keeping the tally had been her job on sorting day for nearly fifty years.

Bob poured himself a cup of coffee and sat at the table with Tommy and Diane. Tommy was unsure whether Diane should be present. Both Bob and Diane sensed this. Bob said, "Tommy, it's OK. Anything you need to tell me she needs to know. If you don't tell her now, she's just going to wait until you leave and torture me until I spill my guts."

Tommy laughed, "She's not going to torture you."

"You think not? You don't know these tough Eskimo women. I saw this one stand bolt upright and empty a forty-five into a charging Grizzly bear that dropped dead so close it slid up to her mukluks before it stopped. You know what she did then? She pulled me out from under the bear and made me pull the sled another dozen miles that day. Then she complained I smelled like an old, dead bear and made me wash myself and my clothes in an ice-cold river. She's mean. Just tell her whatever you have to say now and save me the agony later."

Diane poked Bob in the arm. "You're full of it. That was no ice-cold river; it was a warm spring, and as I recall, you didn't complain."

Bob smiled, remembering the two of them relaxing in the warm spring together. "Yeah, well, OK, but Tommy, she's part of this, so let's hear it."

Tommy was amused and said, "She didn't really do that." Bob and Diane just looked back at him. "Did she?"

They both laughed, "No, of course not."

Tommy was not sure if his leg was being pulled or not. It didn't matter; he had important information to pass on. "First, the county attorney's ruling that your shooting of the two at Adobe Tank was self-defense. That closes the case as far as we're concerned. Unfortunately, the shootout at Adobe Tank, along with the killing of Pollita and the mess with the coyote's abandoned truck, has stirred up the interest of the feds. Not the local Border Patrol or Customs feds, but the Washington feds."

Bob looked annoyed. "What's the feds' interest? Adobe Tank is state trust land. Pollita was found on patented ground. The truck full of illegals was on national forest land, but Border Patrol and the County dealt with that. Sounds like a fishing trip."

"The FBI has expressed some concern that all of it happened on your ranch. They may be thinking there is some criminal involvement on your part, or if not that, it's wild west vigilantism. I'm here to give you a heads up. They're going to question you."

"When will they be here?"

"I don't know. It could be today; it could be next week. They won't call ahead; they'll just show up."

"Has there been any headway on finding out who that bunch at Adobe Tank was?"

The two Mexicans are from Sinaloa. We passed their names to the Sinaloa State Police; all they had on them were their driver's licenses. There was no criminal record for either of them. We can't establish a link between them and any of the cartels."

Bob said disdainfully, "That means nothing. If you asked those cops about El León de la Sierra, they'd say, ¡Quién Sabe!"

"Who?" asked Tommy.

Bob had to consider his answer. "Pedro Avilés Pérez, the boss of the Sinaloa drug business until a few years ago. You remember, he was the Mexican side of the mess at Indian Springs twenty-some years ago." Bob felt a sharp pain as Diane kicked him under the table.

"Someday, Bob, we are going to have to talk," said Tommy.

Bob answered, "Once you're read on, not before." That seemed to settle it, the implication being that it was information Bob had from his days in the army, working with JTF six.

Tommy knew he was going to get no more information on this topic from Bob, so he continued. "The other two were cholos from Phoenix, maybe by way of Los Angeles. Common sense says all of them, including the two from the abandoned truck, are somehow involved with each other, but we can't establish a clear link."

Bob asked, "And still nothing more on Pollita?"

"No, but somehow her murder has to be tied up with this mess."

Bob sat quietly for a few seconds, then said, "Thanks, Tommy. I expect I'm not supposed to know about the feds."

"That's right."

"No problem. They'll never know you were here."

Bob was disturbed by the news that the police in Sinaloa had been notified. "How long ago did you guys contact the Sinaloa Police?"

Tommy pulled out his notepad. "Two days ago. Why?"

"What about the other two from Phoenix. When was the dead one's next of kin contacted, and when did the other one, the driver, make a phone call?"

"Soon, maybe the day after the Adobe Wells shooting incident."

Bob sat back. He and Diane exchanged looks. Bob looked at Tommy and said, "That means both the Phoenix bunch and the Sinaloa bunch know who and where we are. That sucks."

Tommy said, "I don't think it's that bad. You aren't a threat to their business. There's been no repercussions from the two coyotes from the truck."

"That's because they were trespassing on another organization's turf. Those two slugs were lightweights, flying under the radar. If anybody's in trouble with a cartel over that mess, it's those two, not us."

Tommy looked at Diane. He knew all this. He had been trying to spare Diane any additional worry. "I know, just trying to be positive."

Diane was looking at Tommy. "There is no need for you to try and protect me from any of this. Bob and I are in the middle of this. We both need to know what's going on."

"OK, you're right."

Bob then asked Tommy, "Is the rape trial for those two anytime soon?"

"No, the attorneys are asking for more delays. It's the normal way these things go."

"Okay, thanks for the heads up about the feds, and thank you for the information about the rest. We'll be cautious."

+++

The last of the yearlings and cull cows had been loaded, and the big tractor-trailer was pulling away. Tomorrow, the replacement heifers and newly branded calves would be hauled to the old Desert Camp, but now they had a couple of dozen slick calves that had been missed or had been born after the spring works that needed branding.

The propane fire was burning in the branding pot. The irons were getting hot, the syringes were loaded, and the pocketknives had been unfolded and passed over the whetstones. Bob was horseback, as was Gabe; they would be dragging the calves to the fire. Pat was in charge of the ground crew. Bob had set up a dead man for the bulk of the calves, but a few of the larger calves would need to be head and heel roped.

Bob shook out his loop and signaled Gabe to do the same. They started to ease into the calves that were bunched up at the far side of the corral. Bob caught a bull calf by the hocks and was dragging him to the dead man when a car pulled into the parking area. It was a black Crown Victoria sedan.

As one of the ground crew slipped the dead man's loop over the calf's front hocks Bob's horse, keeping the slack out of the rope, turned to face the calf, stepped back and drew the rope taught against the inner tube used as buffer from the dead man to the rope looped around the calf's front hocks. Once the horse stopped, Bob wrapped a couple more dallies on the horn and settled back to wait for the ground crew to do their job.

He had purposely ignored the car and the two suited and neck-tied men who stepped out. By now, they had reached the corral fence and were peeking through the chinks in the juniper corral fence and stretching up on tiptoes, trying to see over it. Shortly, they found a bench next to the fence and stood on it, giving them a clear view of the work going on in the corral.

Bob was enjoying this relatively easy day of work. He had been going for twelve and fourteen hours a day for the past month. This was like a day of rest. A few calves to brand, a shipment to send away, and instructions to pass. Now he had to deal with some foolishness that he neither asked for nor wanted.

Bob sat up and turned to look over his shoulder. "Are you here to proselytize to me or apply for the job of holding down that bench you're standing on?" The two suits looked at each other and said nothing. "Even though you've dressed the part to be on your mission, I expect that's not the case since you're too old. So, if you're not here to convert me to the saints or ask for work, I'm at a loss to know your purpose." The two men looked a bit bewildered. "I'm a busy man, as you can see, so let's hear it."

He was sorry as soon as he said it. They were just doing their job, and here they were in an environment as foreign to them as the surface of the moon. They were staring in disbelief at the bull calf, now steer calf, lying on the ground with a cowboy kneeling on the calf's flank.

The cowboy dropped the calf's scrotum into a coffee can and tossed the calf's testicles to a ranch dog. Then another cowboy put the hot irons to the calf's hip, sending a plume of white smoke up in the air.

After the brand was applied, the first cowboy cut the tip off the calf's left ear. A third cowboy shot the calf with a dose of vaccine. The calf had small horns, so the cowboy with the knife cut them off near the base; the stumps then pumped thin streams of arterial blood into the air. The cowboy with the branding iron traded it for cauterizing irons, held the calf's head still by pressing the calf's muzzle against the ground with his boot, then applied the glowing irons, with not a little pressure to the wounded horn stumps, which sizzled and sent more white smoke into the air. He kept the pressure on until he was sure the bleeding had stopped.

Pat Ochoa called out, "What's that smell?"

Everyone answered, "The smell of burning hair, WOOPHA!" Bob knew that was for the benefit of the dudes that had driven up in the black Crown Vic.

Pat removed the dead man's loop from the calf's front hocks and nodded to Bob. Bob pulled the dallies from his saddle horn and threw slack into his rope. The calf kicked his legs free, stood up, and ran to his mother on the other side of the corral.

Bob then rode over to the fence as he coiled his rope and latched it to his saddle. He introduced himself and asked what they wanted. The two men pulled out their badges and said they were Special Agents with the FBI. The younger agent looked back at the branding crew and said, "That's brutal."

Bob smiled and said, "Do you eat beef?"

"Yes."

Pointing to the work going on in the corral, he said, "Well, that's the beginning of the journey to your plate. Beef doesn't grow in the supermarket cooler. So, are you here to talk to me or someone else?"

"If you're Robert Hasett, we're here to talk to you."

Bob pointed towards the house and said, "By God, you're in luck. That's me. We can go to the house, or we can stay out here, you're call." There was a fair amount of dust being kicked up by the branding crew. The two agents did not hesitate to accept Bob's offer of going to the house and started in that direction.

Bob told Pat that he had to talk to the two feds and to take charge until he got back. Bob then hurried to the house to try and spare the agents from Diane's displeasure. While Bob was annoyed by Tommy's news about the feds coming to question him, Diane was furious. She was not inclined to mask her feelings when it came to family.

The two agents had made their way from the corral to the house and were showing Diane their badges. She was not impressed. She was firmly planted on the porch between the agents and her front door. Her feet were shoulder-width apart, and her arms were folded across her chest. They weren't setting foot in her home.

Bob rode up and stepped down from his horse. He loosened the cinch and threw the get-down rope over the porch rail. Looking at Diane, he could see that going into the house would not meet with her approval. "Gentlemen, let's have a seat here on the porch. That way, I can keep an eye on the branding. Diane, can you bring us some iced tea? I, for one, would like some."

Bob could see that the two men were curious about their surroundings. "It appears you're not from around here," said Bob.

"That's right." Answered the special agent who seemed to be senior.

The younger agent said, "Is anyone from around here. This is the middle of nowhere."

Bob laughed, "This isn't the middle of nowhere. It's not even close to nowhere; it's our home. I once found a place that I thought was the middle of nowhere. It was so remote it made this country look like a sprawling metropolis, but you know what? It wasn't the middle of nowhere. There were people who lived there and called it home. It's all in what you're familiar with, or what you're willing to learn about."

The young agent was not convinced. "I would never fit in here."

"Why?"

The agent smiled at Bob's naivete. "Look at me, I'm way too dark for this country. I'd never be accepted here."

Bob was surprised by this. Just then, Diane and Aunt Maria came outside with a pitcher of tea, glasses, sugar, and lemon slices. Bob said, "Thank you, ladies." Then, addressing the agents, "You've met my wife Diane, and this is my Aunt Maria Barnes." The agents stood and introduced themselves.

Diane and Aunt Maria nodded. Diane had nothing to say. Aunt Maria said stiffly, "Mucho gusto." The women did not offer their hands in introduction and went back into the house.

When Diane and Aunt Maria had left, Bob asked, "Would you like to guess at their ethnic backgrounds?"

The senior agent started to answer, but Bob raised his hand to stop him. He wanted the younger agent to answer, "I'd guess Mexican."

"You'd guess half wrong, Diane's half Eskimo, Mountain Eskimo to be exact, the rest is a mix of Swedish and Koyukon Indian. She'd never been south of the Arctic Circle until she was grown with kids. She's accepted here. My Aunt Maria was born in Sonora, Mexico. She's been on this ranch for over fifty years, and she's accepted here. Look out in that corral. What do you see?"

The FBI men didn't answer. "I'll tell you. A black buckaroo, a Mexican American cowboy, a White Mountain Apache cowboy, and two just plain old honkey, gringo white boys. I have a Mormon camp man over the mountain and a wagon cook of unknown origin. All of them are accepted here. Young man, I found cowboying to be a meritocracy much like the army. If you can do the job, you're accepted. If you snivel and whine, you're out. I encourage you to question my crew if you like."

Bob continued, "That doesn't mean we are without our allotment of prejudiced ass hats in this corner of the country, but there are a lot more decent folks than bigots. Now, what can I do for you?"

The FBI men questioned Bob extensively about what they referred to as the illegals incidents that had taken place on his ranch. They questioned Bob about the death of Pollita, the stranded truck full of illegal aliens, and the shooting at Adobe Tank. After a while, Bob suggested they break for lunch. The two feds discussed this and decided it was not inappropriate if they paid for their meal.

Bob's response to this was, "Good, I'm sure Cookie will be tickled for a few dollars of pocket change." Bob called through the screen door, "Diane, we're going over to the cook house for some lunch. Are you joining us?"

Diane came to the door and said she and Aunt Maria were bringing over dessert. They'd be there soon with sopapillas. She asked Bob to let Cookie know.

As Bob and the Feds were nearing the cook house, Cookie came out on the porch and started beating on a big pan with a steel rod, which he accompanied with a loud grito, that high-pitched shout that is often heard in Mariachi music. The grito begins with a long, high note and ends like a laugh. Bob said to the Feds, "Cookie's showing off."

"Is he Mexican?" asked the younger Fed.

"I don't know, ask him. All I know is he has ID to support his I-9 form."

After a lunch of green chili beef burritos, beans, and rice with sopaipillas and honey for dessert, the crew went back to the corral and finished up. All that was left for the day was cleaning up after the branding and hauling the freshly branded calves to Desert Camp. Bob told Jim to pack up and be ready to move to Desert Camp in the morning. There was a sizable bunch of mother cows hanging around. They were crying out for their weaned calves. In another day or two, they'd drift off. Gabe and John would be leaving in the morning. Another fall works was nearly over.

Bob was standing with the Feds by the corral. "Gentlemen, do you have more questions for me?"

The senior agent said, "It just seems like your ranch is coming in for more than its fair share of trouble. Can you explain it."

"Maybe, come with me." Bob took them into his office, really just an empty room in the barn. On the wall was a map of Tres Cruces with Indian Springs added. He explained the size of the ranch. "This outfit is one hundred sixty-six sections; that's over one hundred six thousand acres. It's nearly twenty miles from east to west and ten miles north to south. It's a lot of country, and some of it's wild. I have three full-time cowboys. We can't possibly police all this on a daily basis, nor do we try, but we do keep the Sheriff and Border Patrol advised of anything we find. I expect if you look at any other area of a hundred thousand acres down here, you'll find it has about the same amount of illegal activity."

He showed them the location of Pollita's killing, the illegals' truck, and the Adobe Tank shoot-out. "One of these, the truck, was on National Forest, Pollita's body was found on a piece of patented ground, and Adobe Tank is on state land. There's half a mountain range and over twenty miles of road between where we found the truck and Adobe Tank, not to mention nearly five months separate the first from the most recent incident. Does that explain it to you?"

They still looked doubtful. "If you'd like, I'll take you on a tour of the ranch to give you a firsthand idea of what we're dealing with. I can see if the Sheriff wants to send someone along with us."

The senior agent said, "That won't be necessary. We'll be in touch if we need more." With that, the agents got in their car and left.

Bob hoped that would be the last he'd hear from the FBI.

CHAPTER SIX

Fort Huachuca, Arizona, October 1995

Bob was sitting at a conference table in one of the new buildings at Fort Huachuca. Gone were the old World War II, wooden stick-built T, for temporary, buildings that had been the mainstay for most of Bob's time at the post. He had spent nine years on Fort Huachuca, scattered from 1970 to 1994. The growth of the fort was substantial with the addition of the Military Intelligence School in the early 70s, but the growth of Sierra Vista was exceptional. Bob remembered Uncle Jack had predicted a big increase in the population of Sierra Vista back in 1971. Bob wondered if his Uncle Jack thought it would grow from fewer than seven thousand to over thirty-five thousand in a span of twenty-four years.

Waiting for the meeting to start, several people were sitting at the conference table. There was a colonel and his sergeant major from the Intel Center, Tommy Judson and his boss, the Cochise County Sheriff, Ivan Gomez from the Douglas Border Patrol station, sitting with the head of the Douglas U.S. Customs Service, a couple of other Border Patrol agents of rank, and what appeared to be their boss, a Border Patrol agent with major general's stars on his shirt, the Santa Cruz County Sheriff, a ranking Arizona State Trooper, assorted municipal cops, some civilians, and what appeared to Bob to be a few feds. Bob was supposed to be representing the ranchers from the border country.

Bob leaned over to Tommy and whispered, "I thought this was supposed to be some sort of planning meeting to establish a working arrangement between different agencies."

"That's the plan."

Bob looked amused and said, "This is far too big a cluster fuck to get anything done. It's going to degenerate into a BOGSATT real fast."

Tommy looked annoyed. He knew Bob could be prickly and impatient with things he considered a waste of time. Tommy said, "It's the first step, Bob. I think it's a positive sign that they're all here. By the way, what's a BOGSATT?"

Bob smiled, "It's a Bunch of Guys Sitting Around a Table Talking. I'm going to sit back against the wall. Wake me when it's time for lunch." Bob saw the look of disapproval on Tommy's face. "Just kidding, I'll stay awake."

"You're not being fair, give it a chance."

Bob said, "OK, I hope you're right. If whoever's in charge can keep people on track, there's hope."

After the initial introductions, there were a few hours of discussion. Some were agency position statements, and one or two were interesting suggestions of merit. As Bob expected, there was a lot of drifting off course into parochial interests, and the requisite number of people trying to impress each other. The meeting inevitably degenerated into near chaos that thankfully ended when some desperate soul called for a bathroom break. Tommy moved back to sit with Bob. "Is this what you meant?"

"Yep. There are more conflicting agendas in this room than at the UN. Only the enforcement and intelligence agencies should be here, and by that, I mean only the ones involved from say, Cochise, Santa Cruz, and maybe Pima counties. All the rest of us civilians and stakeholders should go home."

"Shouldn't you have a voice?"

Bob said, "No. Developing a plan is going to require some change in attitudes from the big agencies, some handholding for the small departments, and a lot of swallowed pride from the bosses, small and large. Agency boundaries will have to be softened, information shared, and in some cases, assets loaned out to other departments. In the end, the peanut gallery, AKA us stakeholders, hold no authority and bear no responsibility for carrying out the plan.

The professionals, like you, carry the burden and are on the blame line. You come up with a plan and brief the peanut gallery on what the plan is. Then, we in the peanut gallery can agree, disagree, or pound sand up our collective butts. In the end, the responsibility, thus the decision, is yours." Bob smiled mischievously and said, "But don't worry, I'll be sure to give you the benefit of my opinion after you've done all the work."

"What do you think will work?"

Bob looked tired. "What will work, probably can't be done. This is a counterinsurgency problem. The military has the assets and knowledge to do this, but without martial law, it can't be done due to the Posse Comitatus Act."

"Yes, I'm familiar with Posse Comitatus, and as I recall, you're familiar with how to get around it. Why can't civilian agencies do it?" Tommy asked?

"All four military branches work for the same Commander in Chief. They have the same Secretary of Defense, and their respective heads sit as the Joint Chiefs. They've been at this multi-service business for decades. They all work within a well-established, well-defined chain of command, yet it can still be like pulling teeth to get them to cooperate with each other."

Bob looked exasperated. "Here you have none of that. You work for the county Sheriff, the troopers work for the governor, and the Douglas PD works for their mayor. Even the border patrol and customs don't work for the same cabinet secretary.

Throw in the FBI, DEA, and whoever else is involved, and you have no unity of command or common agenda. I'm not saying it's impossible, but it will require a lot of time and patience."

Tommy asked, "Any ideas?"

"Start small. Try working something out with the local border patrol and Customs guys. Maybe keep the local PDs in the loop as much as they need to know, but the more people that know, the more likely it is that your plan will be compromised. Don't get too ambitious. Keep the plan simple and flexible. Perhaps most important, and I can't overemphasize this, it is critical to have goals that are definable, measurable, and therefore achievable."

"What about the governor? Should we contact him?" asked Tommy.

"I have no idea. That seems like the state troopers' responsibility. I expect the sheriff would know if it was necessary or even a good idea."

"If the governor's on board, that could mean using the National Guard," said Tommy.

"That might work, but I still think a small start is better. Once you have a workable system and an established hierarchy, you can add players on more favorable terms. The more agencies involved in the initial phase, the more confused and inefficient the operation becomes."

"OK, that's a lot to think about. Are you sticking around?"

Bob stood up, put his hand on Tommy's shoulder, and said, "I have my own kingdom to look after. I can at least have some effect on that. Let me know how it goes." Bob started for the door when he noticed the colonel watching him.

The colonel approached Bob and put out his hand, saying, "Mr. Hasett? I'd like a minute of your time."

"Of course, Colonel, call me Bob."

"The colonel looked at the group milling around the conference room and smiled, "BOGSATT, you called it."

"Yes, sir."

"I heard some of what you were saying to the sheriff's deputy. I'd like your thoughts on this business."

Bob was not crazy about wasting more time, but since he was here and the day was half gone already, he said, "All right, I can give you some time."

"There's an empty office just down the hall."

After the BOGSATT and meeting with the colonel, Bob was driving home. He had repeated all the points he'd made to Tommy. The colonel seemed to agree, at least in principle. "Maybe it'll become something," Bob said to himself. Then he smiled at his own foolishness. Fuck it, don't mean nothin'.

CHAPTER SEVEN

El Paso, Chihuahua, Mexico, April 1996

Andrei Petrov was waiting in a tavern on the south side of Jarez. His contact had him sit in a booth at the back and brought him a cerveza. Andrei sipped the beer and thought, "What's wrong with these people? In America and Mexico, all these people drink beer. Is there nothing better?

Andrei was in Juarez to make an offer to the Juarez Plaza, which was the Chihuahua cartel. He had big ideas and saw an opportunity to rise high in the human trafficking world. He had been involved in the human trafficking business for years, first in Russia and then in New York. He was anxious to make his mark and move up the ladder. He'd had enough of taking orders from people who were dumber than him. Now was his chance.

With a fifteen-hundred-mile permeable border with the United States, and a large population residing on the edge of poverty, Mexico was just waiting for the right man; he was that man. He just needed the cartel to allow him to set up business as their partner.

The bartender came over to the booth and had Andrei follow him. They passed through a door, entering the back room. Five men were waiting for them. The apparent leader of the group introduced himself as El Viceroy, the head of the Jarez Plaza. He asked Andrei to have a seat. Two of the men excused themselves and left. The two remaining men casually took up positions that gave them control of the room. Andrei assessed the situation and decided the four men were sicarios.

After a few polite comments of no importance, Andrei was getting anxious. El Viceroy sensed this. He smiled and said, "OK, my Russian friend, no more small talk. What is your proposal?"

Andrei started to explain in great detail what he wanted to do. El Viceroy stopped him after a few minutes, saying, "I don't need to know the details. Just give me the good stuff. How soon will you start? How much will it cost me; how much will I make?" Andrei answered his questions. After considering what Andrei had to say, El Viceroy told him he'd contact him in a day or two with an answer.

+++

In a small pueblo in the mountains of Durango, Luna Inéz Ortiz López and her little brother Ivan Juan Ortiz López were walking home from school. A large black pickup truck with dark windows turned onto the main road from the drive that led to their house. They stopped and watched as it drove away.

This was not good. The men who drove this truck had been at the house before. They had tried to get Mr. Ortiz to sell his farm, a small holding he received title to when the ejido was broken up by the Mexican government and distributed to the ejidarios. He had had an allotment to graze a dozen head of cattle and a nice parcel of twenty acres of arable land where he grew corn and chilies. It wasn't much, it wasn't even enough to support his family, but it was his.

The men had put a lot of pressure on Luna's father and his neighbors. They weren't interested in the grazing land. All the men wanted was the cropland. They offered all the local property owners money and jobs. If that wasn't enough, they threatened the holdouts' families. Mr. Ortiz was the last to refuse. Luna guessed they'd come back to put more pressure on her father.

The family home was a small four-room house made of stone and timber; common building materials found in the mountains. When the children entered the house, they were greeted by the sight of their mother clutching their baby sister. Both were dead, lying in a pool of blood on the floor. Across the room, tied to a chair, facing the bodies, was Mr. Ortiz. His carotid artery was pumping out the last of his blood.

Ivan ran to his mother, begging her to wake up. Luna went to her father and tried to stop the blood pumping weakly from his throat. She held her hand on the side of his neck, pushing as hard as she dared. Soon, there was no more blood. She realized he was dead. Grabbing Ivan's hand, she ran from the house. They ran to Abuela's house. She would know what to do. Luna was covered in blood, struggling with Ivan, who was in hysterics, making Luna's job more difficult. She fought to keep from breaking down.

They burst into Abuela's house crying and begging for help. She wasn't there. Luna was desperate; she had to get help. Leading Ivan, she ran from the house. There was a house in the pueblo that also served as a small shop. It had a phone. She would go there and call for help.

The passenger in the black pickup truck with dark windows had the driver park at the edge of the pueblo, where the truck would not be seen. He got out and climbed a small berm beside the road. He could see Ortiz's house from here. Soon, two children ran out of the house. He jumped back in the truck and told the driver to go back into the village. These children were the heirs to their father's farm. He couldn't leave them. There had to be no heirs.

The driver asked, "Do we kill them?"

"No, at least not here. That would be too much. It would bring too much press attention. We'll grab them and get out of here."

The truck stopped beside Luna and Ivan. The passenger door was already open. A man stepped out, grabbed Ivan by the arm, and shoved him into the back seat without bothering to open the half door of the extended cab. Holding a gun on Luna, he said, "Get in." Luna thought about running, but that would leave Ivan. She squeezed into the seat behind the passenger. That was the end of April and the end of her childhood.

+++

The next day, they were crowded into the back of an old pickup truck with four other younger girls. They traveled under a tarp in the mountains on back roads. Sometimes there would be a checkpoint. Whenever that happened, one of the men riding in the back of the truck would put his head under the tarp and threaten to shoot the children if they made a sound. There would be a discussion between whoever was in command of the checkpoint and the driver. Luna believed the driver was paying mordida to the authorities. The police or soldiers never looked under the tarp. There were stops where the children were locked in a shed or cellar for a few days. At these stops, some children would be added to the group, and others would be taken away. There might be a change within their captors, with some men leaving and others joining the group.

One thing never changed, at these stops...gang rapes. Luna and any other girl who might be beginning to show signs of entering womanhood were passed around among their captors. After a time, she learned to remove herself from what was happening, at least in her mind. She couldn't stop them, but she could escape into her thoughts. It was how she stayed sane.

CHAPTER EIGHT

Cochise County, Arizona, April 1996

Tommy was sitting at the kitchen table with Bob and Diane. He had called ahead the night before and asked if he could stop by. He wanted to talk to Bob about some moves being made to try and organize the law enforcement efforts along the border. It had been a few months since the meeting at Fort Huachuca. Tommy was no fool, and he thought they were making progress. Bob thought it was worth hearing.

He explained to Bob that the Sheriff and Senior Agent Gomez of the Border Patrol, the colonel at Fort Huachuca, and Gomez's counterpart at Customs had been meeting on a regular basis. They had agreed on a plan to share information. They were to meet in a few days at the fort for something of an official kick-off meeting. Tommy said the colonel had asked that Bob be there.

Bob looked at Diane. She raised her eyebrows and asked Tommy, "What do they want with my husband? He's no cop."

"I know, but the colonel asked that you be there too."

Bob gave Diane a quick look. Nodding his head to her, and said, "OK, Tommy, it can't hurt."

+++

Bob and Diane were sitting at the back of the command lab conference room in Riley Barracks at Fort Huachuca. The law enforcement agencies taking part in the new information-sharing effort were all represented in the front row. The local newspapers, a radio station, and at least one TV station from Tucson were present. There was also a smattering of company and field-grade officers along with some senior NCOs. Among the uniforms were a few familiar faces. Bob recognized one sergeant major as an old friend who was sitting with a chief warrant officer; he had served with both in Vietnam. Bob smiled at them. They smiled back, and the sergeant major gave him a thumbs-up.

He leaned over to Diane and said, "This is like old home week." She just smiled.

Before he could say more, a Major General entered the room. As a Sargent Major called Attention! The general quickly raised his hand and said, "Please remain seated." After everyone had settled down, he acknowledged the law enforcement agencies represented and announced that Fort Huachuca was joining the effort to help with their efforts to share and coordinate information. The joint effort was to be called Operation Hawkeye.

After a brief question and answer period with the press, he nodded to his Sargent Major, who then walked to the back of the room and asked Bob and Diane to accompany him to two chairs in the front row.

Once Bob and Diane took their seats, the general said, "It isn't often that we get the chance to make amends for mistakes of the past. I am indeed fortunate to be able to do that today on behalf of the United States Army. Sargent Hasett, would you and Mrs. Hasett please come stand beside me.

Bob was taken aback. Diane didn't seem so surprised. "Attention to orders," said the adjutant. Then he read the citation dated July 1971 for then Specialist Four, now Sargent First

Class, retired, Robert Hasett. The award of the Distinguished Service Cross, the second-highest award for valor in the United States armed forces, was being presented to Bob for an action that took place on a mountain top in the Republic of Vietnam twenty-four years earlier. The mountain was named Nui Ba Den, and the fight had been brutal. The general took the medal from its box and pinned it on Bob's cowboy vest.

Addressing the room, the general said, "I was a young captain in Vietnam when this battle took place. I can tell you it was a bloody fight. Everyone on that mountain top, whether American or South Vietnamese, was killed or wounded. Only three survived. The general took Bob's hand, leaned forward while shaking it, and under his breath, he said, "Rocky Top's award recommendation for the Medal of Honor is being reconsidered thanks to you."

After the award ceremony, there was a small reception with beverages and pastries. familiar faces in the crowd had come up to Bob to congratulate him on his DSC. They were all genuine, but none more so than the Sargent Major he recognized before the start of the ceremony. Sergeant Major Danny Mohan had waited until the brass had left, then came up to Bob, pumped his hand, and surprised him with a big hug. "God Damn it, Hasett, I told your sorry, dumb ass, twenty years ago that getting this fucking medal was important. Not just important for you, but important for all us pukes that share the danger but don't get shit." Then Danny cracked a true shit eating grin on his face and said, "Can I touch it?"

"Yeah, but you can't sniff it."

+++

On the drive home, Diane said to Bob, "You never told me much about that fight on the mountain."

"There wasn't much to tell."

"Yes, there was. You're a hero."

"I'm no hero, I'm a survivor."

Diane flung her hands out dismissively. "Yeah, and I'm a city-raised valley girl." She got more serious and said, "Don't try and put that 'no big deal' rubbish past me. We both know about being survivors, and that can be tough enough. What I just learned about the man I've been married to for twenty years is that he did more than survive a tough fight; he helped others to get out to safety. You are a hero, and now you have the medal to prove it."

"Hero is an overused word. I'm not about to tell you all those who died were heroes; they weren't. Mostly, we did our jobs; some survived, some got killed. It was all in the line of duty. One was different. He knowingly gave his life. After days of fighting a much larger force, we were overrun. Those of us still alive fell back to the command bunker. We were waiting for the enemy to start rolling grenades through the ventilation shaft or just blow us up with satchel charges. Our forward observer stayed topside in the open and called in artillery on his own position while the rest of us took cover in the bunker. He's the only reason any of us are alive."

Diane noticed that Bob had tears running down his cheeks. She had never seen him cry. "Bob, I'm sorry he's dead, but grateful he helped you live."

"Diane, please don't misunderstand me. I don't have PTSD, nor am I wallowing in self-pity. I don't want anybody's sympathy, but for twenty-four years I've been in debt to that man. I'll never be able to repay the debt I owe him."

"I don't want to hear that nonsense. You repay it every day. You're a good man. You risked your welfare and your life to save me. You adopted my kids and treated them as your own. You've been setting an example for others ever since I've known you. Rocky Top would be proud of you."

Bob was quiet for a while, then said, "The general told me they are reopening his award recommendation for the Medal of Honor. He deserves it."

Diane slid closer to Bob on the Bronco's bench seat and squeezed his arm. "Yes, he does."

+++

Winter had passed without incident, and spring works were over. Bob was riding the Indian Springs country with his Indian Springs camp man, Malachi Snow. Malachi was about to take his family on their two-week annual vacation. They'd be busy traveling between Navajo County, Arizona, and Colonia La Mora, Sonora, Mexico.

They had ridden to the top of a low ridge near the east end of the ranch. Both dismounted. Bob said, "We can take a break here for lunch." Both men hobbled their horses and pulled off their saddles.

Bob was sitting on an exposed rock outcrop, enjoying the view. The country on this part of the ranch was a grassland with a mix of various native grasses and annual forbs. The winter had been kind with enough rain to bring on the cool-season forbs. The country was not yet green, that wouldn't happen until the summer monsoon, but there was an understory of green beneath the cured grasses. On the far side of the San Bernardino Valley were the Peloncillo Mountains and the New Mexico state line. Scattered across the valley were volcanic calderas, old lava flows called malpais, and cinder cones. What was striking was the blanket of golden poppies covering the conical cinder cones rising out of the broad grassland. This was a view Bob always enjoyed.

Malachi walked up and handed Bob a paper bag. "Sariah insisted on packing a lunch for each of us."

Bob smiled, "I wondered what you had stuffed inside that saddle bag."

Malachi looked a little embarrassed. "I don't like to carry so much horseback, but I figured this was an easy day ... so, you know."

Bob said reassuringly, "Yes, I know. Malachi, please thank your wife for me."

"Thank you, I will." Malachi found a spot to sit and eat his lunch. "Bob, as soon as the kids' summer break starts, we'd like to visit some of my family in Navajo County, in Shumway. Then we're going to Colonia La Mora near Bavispe to see Sariah's aunt. I expect we'll be a week at each place. I could stop off here on the way from Shumway to Bavispe."

"That's not necessary, but if you want, just give me contact information for them in case I need to get in contact with you."

"OK."

Malachi, I thought you were from Short Springs?"

"I am, but my uncle is the only family I'm in touch with. He has a small place near Shumway. I don't go back to Short Springs."

Bob knew about Short Springs. He suspected Malachi had been a 'Lost Boy', forced out of the polygamist community by the old men to reduce competition for wives. He had never raised the topic before, but Malachi had just opened the door. Bob asked, "Lost Boy?"

Malachi looked a little surprised and hesitated to answer, but finally said, "Yes, I was lucky, my uncle took me in."

Bob thought this was the point where the line between showing interest in someone versus prying into their private life gets fuzzy. He looked at Malachi for some sign. There was none. Bob decided to say nothing. If Malachi wanted to say more, he would; besides, Bob was well aware that awkward, prolonged silence in a conversation was a pretty effective interrogation technique.

"Your uncle never told you about me?"

"Only that you're a good cowboy, honest and a solid family man. That's all that matters as your boss."

"You know I was raised Mormon," said Malachi.

"I suspected it, your name is sort of a giveaway," said Bob with a smile.

Malachi chucked at that. "What part, Malachi or Snow?"

"Either, but when put together, it's a no-brainer."

"OK, I'll tell you. Sariah and I were born and raised in Short Springs. We'd been friends all our lives, and thought we'd get married someday, but she was supposed to marry the Profit on her fifteenth birthday. I was starting to push against the rules and was getting in trouble with the elders. They were making life hard for me. It was obvious I had no prospects of marrying Sariah or having a family within the church, so we ran away to my Uncle Orrin's. I was seventeen and she was fourteen."

"Didn't they come looking for you?" asked Bob.

Malachi looked amused. "They didn't come looking for me. They were trying to get me to leave anyway. They did try to find Sariah. Uncle Orrin lived up to his name and ran them off. They were genuinely afraid of him."

"His name?" asked Bob.

"He's named after Orrin Porter Rockwell." Malachi looked at Bob to see if that registered.

"OK, you mean like Brigham Young's avenging angel."

"Yeah."

Bob leaned back on his elbows and took a deep breath while taking in the view. Once again, he was surprised by someone's story. There were some amazing people mixed in amongst the normal day-to-day sheep.

Malachi said, "Your aunt and uncle are Mormon, what about you?"

Bob laughed, "I can't even follow the rules to stay in good stead with the Episcopal Church, and that's easy. Some would say I'm no Christian; perhaps they're right, but I do believe. I do know this: I am a radical Pro-tes-tant. I don't like centralized authority in religion. It leads to abuse. I like the idea of parishioners firing their preacher if he or she doesn't measure up.

Bob swept his arm at the view around them. "This is my church. This is God's work. I don't need a structure built by man to commune with God, and I don't want anyone telling me what to believe or how to interpret any gospel. I can read and think for myself. I don't want, nor will I, stand for anyone insisting they are my link to God. I don't need a link. I can and do speak to him any time I want."

Malachi was a bit surprised by Bob's little diatribe. "Bob, what about revelations? You know when someone has a revelation directly from God."

Bob gave Malachi a look that was not sympathetic with this notion. "I run pretty cold on that. It seems to me that most claimed revelations are about telling others how to act or are justifying deviations from the norm. Notice how revelations come from people in power. They result in benefiting the one with the revelation. They are often a tool for control.

Centralized authority in any religion eventually leads to abuse. Look at your case. Sariah was not promised to some old fart by a revelation from God. She was offered as a juicy reward to some staunch supporter of your self-appointed Prophet. That's not God, that's perversion and power."

Bob paused. He was getting hot. It wasn't his place to school Malachi on religion; besides, Malachi had been to a tough school on that topic already. "Perhaps we should leave revelations alone." He smiled and said, "Don't mind me. I'm just a grouchy old doggie. Come on, we have more country to prowl," Bob stood and walked over to his horse.

CHAPTER NINE

Tucson, Arizona, May 1996

The entire Hasett clan, minus grandkids, was sitting in the McKale Center at the University of Arizona. The youngest of Bob and Diane's kids, Carl, was graduating with a degree in history. After the commencement, he would receive his commission in the Army as a second lieutenant of Infantry. Carl's sister Ruth had just completed her residency in OB-GYN and taken a permanent position at the Indian Health Service facility in Fairbanks. Carl's brother, Luke, had flown in from Alaska, where he worked as a wildlife biologist at the Arctic National Wildlife Refuge. He had brought his wife, Joan, and their two small children. Suzie Ochoa had volunteered to watch the kids so Aunt Maria could attend the graduation.

Standing outside after the commissioning ceremony, Diane was looking at her three children. Ruth and Luke were congratulating and ribbing their younger brother. She and Bob gave them some room to enjoy each other's company without parents in the way.

Bob sensed Diane getting emotional. "Are you OK?" He asked.

"I'm fine. Look at them, Bob. We did it. We turned out three wonderful, successful human beings. I'm so proud of them."

"You should be proud of them. You should also be proud of yourself. You're responsible for this."

She looked at him and said, "We are responsible for this."

"Mostly you. Soldiers' wives, at least the good ones, raise soldiers' kids. I was gone too much. You did it."

"You provided them with a role model. Those three know what a man's supposed to be."

Bob smiled and joked, "I'll show you what a man's supposed to be."

She poked him in the arm. "That's big talk for a white boy."

"What, just because I never jackhammered some poor, dumb walrus with an exploding harpoon fired from a giant harpoon gun, I'm not tough enough? I'll remind you; I saved you from a raging porcupine."

"Yeah, OK."

Bob and Diane had arranged to celebrate Carl's graduation with dinner at El Charro's in Tucson. With the newly minted Lieutenant Carl Hasett in tow, the family loaded into the vehicles and headed to the restaurant.

+++

It was getting late when Bob turned off Highway 191 towards the ranch. A pickup with a camper shell was racing east towards them on Sabino Canyon Road. It passed by in a cloud of dust. When Bob looked in his rearview mirror, he saw the pickup's brake lights come on and the vehicle turn to the south on 191. He said to Diane and Maria, "I don't like that. Keep your eyes open for anything unusual along the side of the road, like downed fences, especially at water points."

There had been nothing out of the ordinary until they turned into the ranch drive. The door to the house was open, and someone was lying on the front porch. Bob slid the Bronco to a stop, grabbed his pistol from under the seat, and rushed to the porch. Lying on her face, dead was Suzie Ochoa. Maria and Diane were on the porch right behind Bob.

"Stay here," Bob ordered. He went into the house with his pistol ready. What he found made him grab a wastepaper basket and throw up. Bob never threw up when confronted with dead bodies. Lying on the living room floor with his head crushed was his three-year-old grandson. He shouted, "Stay outside, please."

Diane came in, saw her dead grandson, and asked, "Where's Sandra?"

When confronted with Diane's question, Bob quickly gathered himself and answered, "I don't know." Standing up and starting for the back of the house, he said, "I'll look."

Diane went to the dead child, held his hand, it was warm, holding back the tears, she told herself this is a time to act, the time for tears will come later. "I'll call the Sheriff."

Bob quickly went through the rest of the house in search of his granddaughter. She was missing. He told Diane, who was on the phone with the Sheriff's office, that she passed this on. Not only were there two dead, but there was one missing. Bob heard another vehicle pulling into the yard. That would be his Children, Ruth, Luke, and Joan. Bob rushed to the door. Going down the stairs, he said, "Diane, Aunt Maria, please come with me. We can't let them in."

"I'm staying with Andy," said Diane.

Getting out of the car, Ruth, Luke, and Joan could see Suzie's body. Luke and Joan were frantic to know where their children were. It was all Bob and Maria could do to keep them from rushing into the house. "Andy is gone, Sandra is missing. Please stay here. The Sheriff is on the way. We must maintain the integrity of the scene."

"Gone? What gone?" shrieked Joan. "Where is he? Is he dead?"

"Yes."

"He's my son. You can't stop me." Taking Luke's hand, she said, "We're going in."

Bob knew he should try and keep her away, but this was her son. No power on earth was stopping her from getting to her boy. He lowered his outstretched arms. Then said to his daughter. "Ruth, please come with me."

Joan went to her son, sat next to Diane, who was on the floor holding Andie's hand. She took his other hand and sobbed. Luke stood looking at the mess that had been his boy. He removed his jacket and spread it over the child.

On the porch, Ruth had confirmed Suzie was dead. As she went into the house, Bob whispered to her, "It's bad, be ready."

As soon as she saw her nephew, she let out a small cry but quickly suppressed it. She rushed to him. Lifting the jacket, she felt for a pulse, squeezed Joan's shoulder, and nodded, confirming what everyone knew. Looking at Bob, she asked, "Pops, where's Sandra?"

"I don't know, she's not inside the house. I need to start searching outside. Luke, come with me. You and Carl can help me look." As Bob and Luke went outside, they heard Aunt Maria in the kitchen. Luke looked questioningly at his father. Bob paused. "By God, she's making coffee." Just then, the Sheriff's car pulled in.

+++

Less than two days had passed since the murders of Suzie and Andy, and the kidnapping of Sandra. The bodies would not be released by the coroner for several days or even a couple of weeks. Bob could not wait that long to start out after his granddaughter. He had placed a call to Tommy, asking for whatever information the Sheriff had. Tommy told him he would have something soon.

Carl's car was packed. It was time for him to report to Fort Benning. "Pops, it's not too late. I can get an extension on my leave and stay for a while. You know the Army's not going to have a problem with my asking."

"Thanks, Carl, we appreciate it, but you need to get to Benning. We'll get on here."

Carl led his father away from the others. "Pops, I know what you're going to do. I can help. Let me go with you. We can find her."

"No, you start your life. The Army needs good officers, and I'm not going to let you risk your future. I don't want you anywhere near this. We'll handle it."

"Wait, Pops, do you mean you and Mom are going to deal with this? You're getting too old. Luke and I should be doing this, not you. It should be our business, not yours. Let me stay."

"We have plenty of help. Your mom and Ruth will be here with Joan, and I will have Pat and Luke with me."

Carl continued to protest, "If Luke and Pat go with you, why not me?"

Bob knew he was only trying to help, but he was not going to allow Carl to get involved. "Carl, I know you feel a loss, but trust me, there is no loss that compares to what they're going through. I can't stop them even if I try, and if I don't go with them, they'll wind up dead. Now say goodbye to the others.

As Bob stood watching Carl drive away, the intense grief of the family nearly overwhelmed him. The murder of Suzie was hard on him. The pain of losing Andy and Sandra was crushing him. Luke and Joan were suffering terribly. Pat was taking the murder of his wife really hard. Diane was a trooper, working hard to hold everyone together, but Bob knew she was suffering down deep. Ruth had stepped in, taking on the burden of comforting her brother and sister-in-law. She and Aunt Maria were doing all they could to help relieve the suffering.

On top of the grief of the two murders was the uncertainty of Sandra's fate. Not knowing if she was alive or dead was destroying Joan. Luke tried to help her, but it was his loss too. Bob knew that he would have to go and find her. He wanted to stay for his kids and Diane.

He was starting to feel the years that had piled up on him. This would test him, but there would be no peace for him or any of the family until Sandra's fate was known. He had to at least appear to be holding it together. It was up to him to keep the others focused on the goal. The first task was to find his granddaughter; the second was to deal with the murderers.

Going back inside, he saw dust on the road coming towards the ranch. He waited to see who it might be. He felt for the pistol under his vest. He was never without it now. As the vehicle approached, he stood by the Bronco with his hand on the rifle he kept in it. Bob relaxed; it was a sheriff's car.

Tommy Judson parked and walked up to Bob, carrying two covered casserole dishes. "Bob, there's a pie in the car. Please get it for me." Tommy led the way to the house. When he got to the porch, Diane opened the door. "Diane, the women of the Relief Society from the church sent these."

"Thank you, Tommy. Please pass on our gratitude. Can you stay for a little while?"

"Yes, I have some information." Looking at Luke and Joan, he said, "It's not much, but I want to keep you abreast of the situation."

Diane brought Tommy and Maria ice water; the rest had coffee. Tommy filled them in on some details of what they'd learned, which was very little. He assured them the Sheriff's Office was pursuing every lead. After a while, he asked if he could pray for the family. Aunt Maria knew that Tommy was a holder of the Melchizedek priesthood. She said, "Please do. I know your prayer will be heard; it will be a great comfort to us."

After praying for the family, Tommy excused himself and went to leave. Bob followed him out to his car. Tommy said, "Bob, I didn't tell them, but I have something. You remember there was a trail of blood drops on the steps and the drive. It wasn't Suzie's or either of the kids'. It was the wrong type for Suzie and the wrong RH to be one of the children's. We have no way of knowing whose it is, but we know somebody else was hurt. That's something. Another thing, Suzie had gunshot residue on her hands. She fired a weapon. It may be that she wounded whoever it was that did this. I'm sorry I couldn't tell you this sooner. We just got this from the lab this morning."

"Bob said, Jack's old shotgun is missing. I reported that to your deputies. Anything else? Any idea who they were or where they were headed?"

"Yes, we found a pickup at the border a mile east of Douglas. The registration is bogus. There's lots of blood inside, and an old double-barrel LC Smith twelve-gauge with two spent cartridges in the chambers. Could that be your uncle's gun?"

Bob wondered how long they'd been sitting on this piece of information. "Yes, his was an LC Smith sidelock. He kept a box of federal 7 ½ shot in the cabinet with it."

Tommy said, "That's something. Can you get me that box of cartridges? Maybe we can match them to the spent rounds in the gun."

"Of course, I'll be right back."

When Bob returned with the box of cartridges, Tommy said, "We lifted prints off the truck. There was one small set; it could be your granddaughter's. There were several others, but two were more prevalent than the others. One on the driver's side, steering wheel, door handle, stuff like that. The other was on the passenger side. That's where most of the blood was. We didn't get a hit on the passenger side prints, but we did on the driver's side. His name is Pedro Grijalva. Apparently, he's a US citizen with family in Sonora. He's currently on bale awaiting trial for a drug dealing charge. The gang cops believe he's associated with the two cholos you had the run in with at Adobe Tank. They have him on their radar."

Bob shook his head. "Outfuckingstanding, you've got to love the system. Well, now he's on my radar."

"Bob, don't take this into your own hands. The FBI has already got their eyes on you. Let us handle it."

"The FBI can pound sand up their collective butts. I recommend they use a stout mallet to pack it tighter, God damned dilettantes."

Tommy nodded his head, then said, "The colonel wants to meet with you today. He wouldn't tell me anything." He pulled out his notepad and continued, "He wants you to meet him at the SSO. Here's his number, call him to set it up."

"Thanks, Tommy."

"I know this must be hard. Maybe even harder than Angelina. Can I do anything?"

"Just keep after it."

"I'm so sorry, Bob. If I can help in any way, I mean in any way, just ask."

Bob thought about this. It reminded him of a conversation he'd had with his uncle as he was heading out to hunt down the Indian Springs crew. He had said something about keeping his uncle out of it so he could maintain deniability. Uncle Jack had told Bob in no uncertain terms that he didn't need deniability; he was Bob's uncle, and Angelina, being Bob's wife, made him her uncle too. Uncle Jack made it clear; he was part of it. Bob wondered if he could trust Tommy Judson as far as he'd trusted his Uncle Jack. He decided even if he could, it was asking too much of Tommy. "Thanks, Tommy. We'll get by."

"OK, Bob, our prayers are with your family. Keep me posted." With that, Tommy Judson got in his car and left. Bob went back into the house and called the colonel.

+++

Bob was standing outside what they used to call the Green Door. It was the entrance to the Special Security Office (SSO). He rang the bell and looked up at the camera. He heard the door click, and a young female NCO opened it. She stepped out and asked, "What's your name?" Bob told her and handed her his US Army retired ID. She consulted a clipboard and said, "OK, come with me."

She escorted him to the front desk, where he signed in and got an "escort required" visitors badge. She then took him to a small conference room and said the colonel would be in soon. Bob took a seat and waited. He'd last been in the SSO when he was clearing post to retire, being read off the sensitive intelligence programs. He was not currently read on to anything in the SCI world. He thought his Special Background Investigation might still be current, but that meant nothing without being in a billet and being read on. Damn, thought Bob, I'm glad to be done with that alphabet soup rubbish.

The colonel walked in and held out his hand. "Good afternoon, Mr. Hasett."

"Good afternoon, Colonel. Please call me Bob."

"Bob, it is. Call me Ken."

"Sure, Colonel."

The colonel smiled, "Old habits."

Bob nodded, "Yes, Sir."

"Did you bring your recall orders?" Every Army retiree was required to have recall orders that stayed in effect until his or her sixtieth birthday. If a retiree didn't accept the recall orders, they would not receive retired pay. It was a policy unique to the military.

"Yes, Sir." Bob pulled a folded copy of his orders from his inside vest pocket.

The colonel looked them over and said he'd need to make a copy. Bob told him to keep them; he had more copies at home.

The colonel produced a document from a manila folder. It was Department of Defense Standard Form (SF) 312. "Bob, I need you to read this and sign it. I know you are familiar with all this, but in accordance with DoD regulation 5200.1-R we need to do it. It makes it legal for me to share this information with you." Bob read the familiar form and signed it.

The colonel then pulled out some other documents from his folder. They had been heavily redacted and marked as Secret No Foreign, Exempt from the General Downgrading Schedule. While the sanitized information on the documents could not be attributed to a source due to the redactions, the intelligence was exceptional. Bob looked up at the colonel. "Colonel, this is excellent information. Are your people prepared to act on it?"

"No, neither is anyone else, at least not without notifying the Mexican government, and you know how that will turn out."

"Has this been made available to Hawkeye?"

"No, it's too sensitive. If this got out to the press, we'd be shut down instantly. I'm letting you see it because you know how to handle classified data. I also believe that this problem needs to be dealt with. What they did to your family, on our side of the border, is horrible, it's unacceptable. It will happen to others if we can't stop it. I'm providing this to you because you've proved over and over that you're self-reliant."

Bob was surprised by the tone of the colonel's comments. The implication was pretty clear. "Can I have some time to study this information?"

"Yes, but you can't copy anything down. I can make a map of the area in question available to you."

"Yes, Sir, that would be a big help."

"I'll be back with the map." When the colonel reached the door, he turned around and smiled at Bob and said, "Your cousin, Scotty, said to tell you hello."

Bob had called Scotty the morning after the attack on his family. After the colonel left, Bob said to himself, "That explains a lot." His cousin Scotty Cooper had been a Special Forces officer for most of his thirty-year career. He'd retired in the mid-eighties. He'd worn the green beret since Christ was a corporal. Even though he was retired, he kept his hand in. The special ops world was a small, tight-knit bunch. Bob would have to give Scotty a call.

The information Bob was reading had two plus one going to Agua Prieta the night of the murders and kidnapping. The two being adult males, and the plus one being a child. They had remained in Agua Prieta for at least twenty-four hours. It was suspected that they were getting medical treatment from a veterinarian who had a reputation for treating people without notifying the police.

Bob was poring over the map while he read the reports. It said several calls were made to someone in the town of Bavispe. He remembered Cruz talking about Bavispe. He also knew that there was a fundamental Mormon colony in that area with family ties to his Indian Springs camp man. That might be helpful. Continuing with the reports, there was chatter indicating they might go east to Chihuahua.

The colonel entered soon, carrying a push-to-talk phone. He plugged it in and said, "You have a call."

Bob answered, "Hello."

The voice on the other end was his cousin Scotty. "Hi Bob, first, I want to tell you how sorry Barb and I are about the tragedy your family is going through."

"Thanks, Scotty."

"Ken filled me in on the basics of what he knows. He's a good guy; I've known him since he was a rookie Lieutenant in Vietnam. You can trust him."

"OK, Scotty, that's good to know."

"I want you to write down this phone number and call it from a public phone. Do it soon."

"Rodger, Scotty, I'm on it."

"Bye, Bob, I'll stay current on this. Good luck."

As soon as Bob was off post, he stopped at a public phone in Sierra Vista and called. It was a local number. The female voice on the other end said they needed to meet at the city park.

Bob asked, "How will I know you?"

"Don't worry, I'll recognize you. Pick out a picnic table with no one close by and wait."

Bob was sitting at the picnic table when a woman approached him and said, "Hi Bob, I'm Jane." She didn't offer her hand; she just sat down at the table across from him. Bob thought there is nothing about this woman that stands out. She is of average height, has an average figure, brown hair of medium length, a pleasant but unremarkable face, and her clothes are business casual. There is absolutely nothing to make this woman do anything but blend into a crowd. Bob thought she's perfect for human intelligence. Good humint types were everyman or everywoman, they're not James Bond.

Jane continued, "I've brought myself up to speed on your situation. I'm here to act as the conduit between you and our sources. Other than that, we are very limited in what we can do once you cross the fence. Do you understand?"

"Yes."

"You have my number if you need to contact me. Use it to pass me regular sitreps, let's say every forty-eight hours. You do know what a sitrep is?"

Bob was amused by the question. "Despite my country bumpkin attire, I do have an intel background. So, unless you three-letter agency types have changed acronyms in the past three years, I expect it still means situation report."

"Three-letter agency, is it?"

"Yeah, TLA."

She flashed a very slight smile. "I heard you could be a smart ass."

"Some say it's my finest feature. I think they exaggerate." Bob then asked, "What if I'm unable to get to a phone in forty-eight hours?"

"I'll hold off for another forty-eight hours. If you miss two sitreps, I must consider notifying the extraction team. I'll play it by ear."

"Fair enough."

Jane continued, "One of the men you're looking for is named Grijalva. He's pretty low-level. He falls between a falcon or coyotes and a sicario. He's nasty, but not be very experienced or bright."

Bob was impatient to get started. He held up his hand and interrupted. "I'm sorry, this is not an intel brief to some DC bureaucrat holding the purse strings. I don't need a lot of background or justification. I only need to know where they are and where they're going; names and contacts would be nice."

"OK, the short version is that they seem to be crossing from the Sonora side run by Miguel Ángel Caro Quintero to the Juárez side run by Amado Carrillo Fuentes. We don't know if their bosses are aware of what's happening. This kind of cooperation between cartels doesn't happen in the drug business, at least not since the breakup of the Guadalajara Cartel and the demise of Miguel Ángel Felix Gallardo. This is new and disturbing if it signals a possible alliance between Chihuahua and Sinaloa. Hopefully, that's not the case and they're just going rogue."

Impatiently, Bob said, "Go on."

She pulled a small sheaf of papers from her handbag. Passing them to Bob, she said, "These are one-time use code sheets. They work like the CEOIs you had in the Army. Each one is good for a single phone call. Just use them in the order in which they are numbered. Once you use one, burn it. I will use them for decoding any sensitive data I send to you. You are to use them for any sensitive information you are sending to me. If a coded message is to be sent, it is to be preceded by the statement, 'Prepare to copy.' When the receiver is ready to receive the message, the response is, "Send it.' Then the coded data will be sent by coded phonetic alphabet in five-letter groups."

Bob nodded his understanding, but something was bothering him. She assumed he was on board. He didn't know what it would cost him. He was sure there was a price. "I'm grateful for the support, but for the life of me, I don't understand why you're helping a private citizen recover his granddaughter. This is way outside any TLA's area of interest."

Jane sat back and took a deep breath. She was obviously trying to determine how much to tell Bob. Finally, she asked, "Does it matter?"

"God damned right it matters. I need to know who I'm in bed with. I don't care what agency you're with. What's your game?" Can I trust you?

"OK, we're concerned about what's happening between Sanora and Chihuahua. There are indications of cooperation in a new venture. We are guessing the new venture is human trafficking, but that's not confirmed. With the evidence that your granddaughter was most likely taken to Sonora, this may be a link. One of the names involved in your granddaughter's abduction is part of Caro Qintero's Sanora cartel. Disturbingly, we have seen his name come up in chatter from Jarez. That contact between cartels hasn't happened since the breakup of the Guadalajara cartel.

Bob asked, "If I accept your help, what's expected of me?"

"All I want is for you to tell me what names you come across."

"So, if I accept, I give you names, or whatever cartel information I stumble across, right?"

Jane said, "Yes."

"And will you provide me with operational support and intel?"

"Yes."

"Okay, if shit goes tits up, can I count on you to cover my back? If the bosses want to scape goat my ass, will you stand in the door and take a HEAT round for me?"

Jane was taken aback by Bob's challenge. "Yes, of course."

"Are you sure? I would hate to be hung out to dry or be sacrificed to the gods of National Interest."

"I won't allow that to happen."

"You sound pretty sure of yourself. This could get really messy. Are you willing to accept the risk of having me as your responsibility?"

Jane was about to ask if the roles were reversed, would he do all that for her? She decided not to ask; however, she did ask, "If I'm supposed to take a heat round for you, I need to know what it is."

Bob smiled and said, "It's an acronym HEAT for a High Explosive Anti Tank round."

"Ouch, I guess I'd only have to take one."

"Yep, one's the limit. So, if we're going to play together, it's as a partnership, right?"

"Well, yes, I expect so."

"Fair enough."

"If you're satisfied with this arrangement, I'll give you a data dump on what I know." Bob nodded and settled back. Jane added, "This is all to be committed to memory, no notes."

Bob said, "Roger, let's hear it."

After the meeting at the park, Bob hurried home. He had excellent intelligence, a decent map, and a point of contact for intel updates. Most importantly, he had a plan.

CHAPTER TEN

Borderlands, United States and Mexico, Late May 1996

Bob had taken steps to protect his family and his employees even before he met with the colonel and got the intelligence download. He'd asked Malachi to send his family to a safe place. Malachi had willingly complied, sending them to stay with family in Shumway, Arizona. Bob had moved Jim, Malachi, and Gabe into the bunkhouse at headquarters. He had insisted on this, as he said, "There's strength in numbers." He had also strongly recommended that the cowboys go about their business on and off the ranch armed. Additionally, they were to travel in groups and never alone, which meant a lot more gas expenditure since they would be hauling themselves and their horses to and from the camps. Bob understood that all this was inconvenient for the cowboys and added a level of inefficiency, thus costing the ranch operation, but it was essential to ensure everyone's safety.

Bob needed someone to cook for the crew. It was more than he would ask of Diane or Aunt Maria under the circumstances. He got word to Cookie, who agreed to return, with the additional benefit of adding another gun to the crew. Bob never had any doubt about Diane's steadfastness in the face of danger, nor did he question her or Johann's skill with firearms. He had faith in their ability to protect themselves, but he felt better with the crew at headquarters. Now there would be substantial firepower at headquarters.

Bob had met with Tommy on his way home from the meeting with the colonel and Jane. He said he would appreciate the Sheriff's Office checking on his family and crew. The more visible, the better. "It's not about catching anybody, it's about dissuading them," Bob said.

Tommy assured him the Sheriff's Office would have a frequent and very visible presence on the ranch. He added that he would contact the Border Patrol, the Brand Inspector, the local Game Warden, and the Douglas District Ranger of the Coronado National Forest. He felt sure they would be willing to increase their presence.

Now it was time for Bob to talk to the family and fill them in on the latest information and what that meant to them. With him at the dinner table were Diane, Luke, Joann, Ruth, Aunt Maria, and Pat. He gave them a sanitized, very general version of the information he had received. First, he said Sandra was alive. He avoided any details but told them he had a pretty good idea where she might be and where she was being taken. He said he was leaving in the evening, after supper.

Pat and Luke both stood and demanded that they go with him.

Bob said, "No. I don't need armatures getting in the way. I strongly encourage you to stay here and look after the family." He knew he was going to lose this argument, but he had to try.

Pat said, "Suzie was my family, my wife. I'm going. If I have to, I'll follow you. You can't stop me."

Luke was just as adamant about going. "Sandra is out there. She's my daughter. You can't stop me."

"If you two insist on going, you will do as I say. Is that understood?" They said they understood and would follow his lead.

Bob didn't know how long they would be gone, but he told Diane he would check in with her periodically. "Diane, you've got a big job ahead with the family. Why don't you let Malachi handle the day-to-day ranch work? She looked at him and nodded. He added that while he was gone, there would be an increased law enforcement presence on the ranch.

All these people sitting around the table were family. Even Pat, who was not officially related, but had been a friend for over twenty years and was Cruze's son-in-law. He decided he could trust them with the plan. "You must keep what I'm about to say between only us." Everyone agreed. "We're going to Agua Prieta to find the veterinarian's office of a guy named Cardenas. Apparently, he's treating the murderers for wounds. If we find them there, we'll be home with Sandra tomorrow. If not, we'll learn what we can and continue to search."

Luke asked, "When we find Sandra, what about the murderers?"

Bob answered, "The official party line is we turn them over to the authorities."

This elicited a hostile reaction from both Luke and Pat. "Are you shitting me!" said Pat.

Bob looked at them in such a way as to arrest any protest. "That's the official party line. Are either of you official party members?"

"No," answered Luke and Pat.

"Well then, I wouldn't lose any sleep over it. Get your gear, we leave after supper."

When Luke and Pat went to load their gear in the ranch truck, Ruth asked her father, "Pops, can I come with you, at least to the veterinarian's clinic? I can help if this guy needs medical attention."

"I appreciate your offer, but no. If I cared at all about this guy's future, I'd consider taking you, but I'm not risking anyone for this ass hole. Besides, you are beholding to the Hippocratic oath; I'm not. I don't want to put you in an untenable situation."

"You're taking Pat and Luke. Am I not allowed to go because I'm a woman?"

Bob put his hands on her shoulders and looked into her eyes. "The last I checked, your mother's a woman, and there is no one on the planet I'd rather have with me when shit hits the fan. You're definitely your mother's daughter, and I know you'd be a big asset, but like your mother, you're too valuable to risk on something as simple as this. I need you to be here for your mother and Joan. That's going to be the hard task.

He could see that Ruth was not altogether convinced. He took her hand and said, "I'm not taking Luke and Pat because their men. I don't need them for this, and if I could leave them behind, I would. They'll likely be more trouble than help, but I can't stop them from going. If I don't take them with me, they'll go on their own and get killed."

Ruth knew her dad was right. As a girl, she'd heard the hushed rumors about the disappearance of the Indian Springs crew. She knew about what her dad and her mother had gone through on the tundra. He'd been a soldier for most of his life. She, therefore, had no doubt about his ability to handle himself or control the others, but she was worried all the same.

She knew there had to be a breaking point. After all he'd been through over the years, he had to be close to it. The years had to have taken a toll. Now his grandson was dead, and his granddaughter had been kidnapped. No one could deal with all this and not be affected. She asked, "How about you, Pops. How are you?" She pointed at his heart and asked, "In here? Then, "pointing to his head, "in here?"

Bob sighed, "Not worth a shit, but I don't have any choice. I need to hold it together, at least until we get Sandra back. After that, we'll see."

"Is there anything I can do?" she asked.

"Yes, do what you've always done, be strong, and be steady."

"Sometimes that's an act, Pops."

"Of course it is. That's when it's hardest and most important. I know you've got this."

The phone rang, and Diane answered. She brought Bob the phone. "Hi, Bob, it's Scotty. Just a quick update. An A team from the 10th SF group is scheduled to start their annual two-week desert training. They're tired of going to Fort Huachuca all the time. They're looking for new country, they asked if they could use the ranch this year."

"Of course. When?"

"Day after tomorrow," answered Scotty.

"What do they need from us?"

"Nothing."

"If they need anything, have them contact Diane."

"Roger."

Bob knew this was Scotty's doing, and he knew it was to protect his family. "I can't thank you enough."

"No sweat, GI. Remember to keep your head on a swivel, aim for center of mass, and don't stop pulling the trigger until they stop twitching."

"Will do."

+++

It was midnight. Bob, Luke, and Pat were at the side door of Cardenas's veterinary clinic. There was no sign of any activity inside. Bob tested the doorknob. It was locked. He was considering breaking the glass window in the door and reaching in to unlock it when Pat touched his arm, pointed at a window, and whispered, "I can get in there."

The window was small and about eight feet off the ground, but it was cracked open. Bob nodded at Pat and said, "OK, we'll give you a boost."

Soon they were in the clinic. Using a red-filtered flashlight, they moved from room to room. Finally, they found their man in a small side room that had been made up into a makeshift treatment room. Seeing there were no outside windows or doors in the room, they turned on the light. They could see that Suzie had made him pay. His right arm had been amputated just below the shoulder. There was a lingering odor of decay about him. It seemed the vet was not wasting money on large doses of antibiotics.

Pat started to reach for him. Bob stopped him and said, "Wait, we need information. He's no good to us dead."

Pat was not happy, but grudgingly gave in and said, "Alright."

Bob began to interrogate, with Pat interpreting. This was too important to risk a misunderstanding due to Bob's limited Spanish. The thug called himself Chico Soto. He claimed he was a big-time Sicario in a powerful cartel. Bragging like this was a sure sign he was way down the food chain. He was scared and trying to convince them he was too important to mess with. Bob laughed derisively and said, "Sicario, my ass, more like Sicarrito."

After some rough handling, Soto revealed that his partner was Pedro Grijalva, and he had also caught some pellets in the leg from Suzie's shotgun. His wounds were bad enough to hinder his movement, but not so bad that he couldn't move on after Cardenas had treated his leg. He stayed in Agua Prieta only long enough for his brother to arrive. The Grijalva brothers left and took the young gringa to Bavispe. When asked why they had attacked his family, Soto said, "It was payback."

"For what?" Demanded Bob.

"For you getting in the way."

Bob asked what the brothers planned to do next. Soto decided he had said enough and refused to answer. Bob poked his stump and asked again. Soto proved to be pretty free with his secrets, with only a little persuasion. He said the brothers planned to cross the Sierra Madre from Bavispe, Sonora, to Chihuahua. Diego Grijalva, Pedro's brother, had already arranged to take a couple of children he had locked away near Bavispe to a hacienda near Sierra de Enmedio. The plan was to collect a few more children there and go on to Janos, where El Chino would take over and get them across the border. The addition of Sandra was an unexpected bonus.

"Who's El Chino?" Bob asked.

"I don't know, just El Chino."

Bob poked Chico's stump hard. "Who is El Chino?"

Chico's scream was stopped by Pat's hand over his mouth. When he had recovered enough to speak, he said, "His name is José Wong. Everyone just calls him El Chino."

Bob pointed at Chico's stump and said, "What else?"

Chico didn't hesitate to answer, "He is el jefe for the Janos Plaza."

"Is the Janos Plaza dealing in people now?"

"Yes."

"Are they going to drive back this way to go around the Mountains to Sierra de Enmedio," asked Bob?

"No," answered Chico. "They are going to cross the Sierra."

"Why?"

"Because they are doing business with El Chino. He is Juarez cartel; this is Sinaloa cartel country. They are breaking the rules. Driving on the highway is not safe for them. They have to keep it secret."

"Is there a back road over the mountains?"

"Maybe, I don't know."

"Thank you, that information is a big help to us." With no expression of malice or anger, Bob pointed at Pat and said, "El es esposo de mujer muerta," then, pointing at Luke, Bob said, "El es padre de niño y niña," and finally, pointing to himself, he added. "Y estoy amigo de mujer muerta e abuelo de niños."

A few minutes ago, Soto had begun to feel he might survive the night, now looking at Bob, he knew he would not. He crossed himself with his remaining hand. Bob sent the others to the truck. This was no time for emotion or rookies.

As they got into the truck to leave, Pat said, "Bob, your Spanish sucks."

Bob answered with no conviction. "That's quite distressing. I'll be sure to work on it."

"Sicarrito was a nice touch, did you just make that up?"

"Yep."

+++

It would be light soon. They were on the Arizona side of the border at a pay phone in Douglas. Bob placed two calls. First, he called Jane, then he called Diane.

He told Jane what he'd learned from Soto. He told her he was starting for Bavispe as soon as he was off the phone. He would contact her from there with anything new. He said he wanted to send his wagon cook, Cesar Robles, to Janos in a few days. It was important to have someone at that end in case he couldn't catch Grijalva before he got there. She said that wasn't necessary; she'd have her contact deal with it.

"That's a switch," said Bob. "I thought you couldn't get that involved."

"It's a fluid situation. We must stay flexible."

"Semper Gumby," said Bob. That was sitrep number one.

He then called Diane and told her they had found out what he needed. They were headed to Bavispe. He thought they'd be heading over the Sierra Madre by the afternoon. He'd keep her posted when he could, but it might be a few days.

+++

Bavispe was a small town of about seven hundred inhabitants. The name came from the Opata Indian word Bavipa, meaning where the river changes direction. Life in Bavispe had not changed much in nearly three hundred years. People went to mass on Sunday, were baptized, married, and buried in the church. Every year, they looked forward to the festival celebrating their patron saint, the archangel San Miguel. They relied on the priest to see to their spiritual needs, the alcalde to see to their town, the police to protect them, and they worked their land.

They farmed along the river bottom, where they grew corn, beans, chili, and hay. They grazed their cattle, horses, mules, and burros in the mountains and on the alluvial fans that extended down from the mountains. They hunted deer, turkey, and small game. They gathered medicinal plants to treat illness and injury for themselves and their livestock. Bavispe, like much of rural Mexico, was tied to the earth.

Bavispe had begun as a Jesuit mission. In the 17th century, the church was bringing the cross and salvation to the local Opata Indians whether they wanted it or not. Over time, a presidio was built to protect against Apache and Comanche raiders, but in 1887, the presidio, mission, and in fact the rest of Bavispe were destroyed by an earthquake that was so strong it flooded the mines in Tombstone, Arizona, over a hundred miles away.

Life on the northern frontier of Mexico was hard. It had always been a dangerous place to live with frequent Apache and Comanche raids, gringo filibusters trying to establish their own kingdoms, and the frequent revolutions and coups that disrupted any political stability that might have existed. Now the Frontera was falling under a new threat.

Many of the past hardships had been brought by people who at least had some sort of code. The church thought it was doing good by bringing salvation and civilization to the Indians. The numerous political upheavals claimed, rightly or wrongly, to be necessary for the improvement of the country and its people. In the case of the Apache and Comanche, small raids on their neighbors were an essential part of their economy. The taking of a few horses, children, or women added resources to their limited supply. As bad as all this was for the local inhabitants, and it was, none of it held a candle to the new threat.

The cartels had no intention of improving the lot of their people or their country. Money was not their primary motivator; it was their only motivator. The cartels were devoid of any scruples, honor, or accountability. If organizations can possess mental traits, then the cartels were sociopathic. They were truly evil. Even a village as far off the beaten track as Bavispe could not escape their influence. The people noted the increased vehicular traffic passing through from the south. Some of their young men were now driving fancy pickup trucks that were far more expensive than their means. Strangers were now more common than before; unwelcome change was in the air.

Bob, Pat, and Luke arrived in Bavispe early in the afternoon. Bob found his contact, Jorge Castro. They met in a small riverside park north of town. Jorge explained that Pedro Grijalva had strong ties to the Sinaloa cartel, fancying himself as a sicario. He'd arrived a day ago, walking with a severe limp using a cane. He and his brother Diego had not been seen in town since yesterday afternoon.

Jorge asked Bob, "Do you know someone named Snow?"

"Yes, I have a cowboy named Snow."

"Does he have relatives here?"

"His wife does."

Jorge said, "That group mostly keeps to themselves, so please hold this close."

"Of course." Answered Bob.

"First, they would never have contacted me if not for the snow family relationship. They know what happened on your ranch, so they have been watching. The Grijalva brothers left yesterday. My contact didn't know where they were headed, but they went east, pulling a stock trailer with horses and mules into the Sierra. That makes sense, they'd have to be horseback or on foot to cross the Sierra Madre." Jorge explained that the heavy La Niña rains of two winters ago had washed out the over-mountain track in many places, making it impassable for vehicles. Jorge had more news. Jane said there was confusing chatter with the Grijalvas about a pickup at Sierra de Enmedio or Janos.

Bob considered what he had for intelligence. Soto said they were not taking the highway and that they were meeting someone in the Sierra and going on to Sierra de Enmedio in Chihuahua to deliver their cargo to somebody called El Chino. Jorge's source said they were seen going east into the mountains with horses and mules. This confirmed Soto's story about going to Chihuahua. Joan said there was chatter about them meeting a contact in either Sierra de Enmedio or Janos. A second confirmation of the Chihuahua link. Despite the animosity between the Sinaloa and Chihuahua cartels, it was clear that the brothers were on their way to Chihuahua.

Bob knew he was headed into the Grijalvas' home country. They'd been smuggling drugs to the US through these mountains for decades. It would be difficult to get the drop on them, but there was no choice. Time was critical. The Grijalva boys had a day on him. He had to start now.

The Mormons of Colonia Morelos provided them with horses and tack, along with two pack mules. Jorge trailered them up the road as far as he could until they came to a washout. Here, Pat and Luke were unloading the animals from the trailer while Jorge and Bob unloaded their gear. Jorge looked at the firearms they had brought. There was Bob's old Swedish Mouser, an M16, and Bob's old Model 1911 45 pistol. Luke had Jack's old

243, and Pat had brought his 3030 and an old single-action 45 revolver. Jorge said, "It looks like you're ready for war."

"If necessary."

"Well, I expect you know what you're doing. I'll update Jane when I get back to Bavispe. Anything you want me to tell her?"

"Yeah, tell her I should be able to catch up with them soon."

"I can do that," said Jorge. He held out his hand and said, "Vaya con Dios y suerto con todos."

Bob took Jorge's hand and answered, "Gracias con todos y ¡Mucha Suerte!

CHAPTER ELEVEN

Sierra Madre, Northern Mexico, May 1996

After a few hours on the trail, they were at the bottom of a particularly steep slope that they had to climb. Bob had dismounted and had the others do the same. He needed the horses to last. "We'll be footback for a while." He pushed them hard up the steep switchback trail to the top of the ridge. Pat and Luke were young and strong; they may complain, but they were doing fine. He, on the other hand, was blowing like a steam engine. His age and old wounds were making themselves known. "This is no hill for a climber," he said to himself. Then, to help maintain his pace and occupy his mind, he started reciting old Army cadences in his head. "Up the hill, so good; Down the hill, no good; Through the hill, ha, ha; THROUGH THE HILL, Aaaagggg; and so on. It was a useful distraction.

At the top of the ridge, Bob stopped, telling the others to take a break. They were still on the west slope of the Sierra. The trail was the old Overmountain Track, now disused due to impassable washouts. Up ahead, it started side-hilling down a steep slope that formed the south side of a deep canyon.

He could see hairpin switchbacks at places where the slope was near vertical. The trail eventually crossed the canyon and then climbed up the other side, where it topped out on the crest of the spur. According to the map Jorge gave him, it should stay on the ridge top for a short distance before dropping down into another canyon and following it to the northeast for a few miles.

There was still a lot of steep climbing to do over rough country before reaching the top of the mountain range. The sun was setting. The trail ahead was unfamiliar to him. He considered it too risky to attempt in the dark. Bob decided to stop for the night. They would get an early start in the morning. They'd be on the move with the beginning of morning twilight.

He pulled the saddle off his horse, Pepe, and told the others, "We're camping here tonight." There wasn't a nearby water source, but the stock had tanked up from a drinker on the trail a couple of miles down the trail. Indicating the horses and mules, he said, "I'd like to water these guys tonight, but they should be OK until we reach water in the morning. I expect there's some in that canyon bottom ahead." Once the horses and mules were hobbled, they began stripping beans from some small mesquite trees. Bob knew that tomorrow he'd push hard. He hoped the horses were up to it. He expected they'd have to lead them part of the time, not trivial in steep terrain. 'Oh well, suck it up, old man.' He thought.

Bob passed out MREs. "You guys are in for a real treat. These are the army's replacements for C-rations. The name MRE is the abbreviation for Meals Ready to Eat. My soldiers said it really meant Meals Rejected by Ethiopia." Reading the printing on his envelope, he said, "Mine's Chicken ala King. It isn't great, but it's a lot better than most. They may taste like crap, but they are balanced and have lots of calories. Two a day will be plenty for us." In Bob's opinion, none of the MREs measured up to C-rations; even his least favorite C-ration, ham and eggs, was better than most MREs.

Bob laid out his bed away from the other two. He felt the need for some privacy. Sitting on his bedroll, he was using what evening twilight remained to glass the area ahead. He thought he might see something. On the far side of the canyon, where the trail neared the top of the opposite ridge, he thought he saw a light flicker. He could tell nothing more about it and was not even sure he had really seen it.

After it got to be full dark, the flickering light continued, but there was nothing else he could see. It would have to keep until morning. He tucked his boots under his bedroll, rolled up his jacket to use as a pillow, loosened his clothes, put the M16 within easy reach, and the pistol under his makeshift pillow. Once he was satisfied, he'd done everything he laid back, pulled his covers over him, and stared up at the sky. Bob was no stranger to sleeping out in the open, but this time it was hard.

The sky was black with no moon. The air was crystal clear with no haze or dust. The stars were so bright he felt as if they were close enough to touch. He remembered a scene from a movie he'd seen recently where Hawkeye is explaining how the stars are the souls of the departed. Bob looked at the stars and wondered if little Andy was one of them. Maybe Angelina, Jack, Suzie, Cruz, and Diane's stillborn baby were up there. Perhaps one day, he and Diane would be stars. He decided he liked that. Somehow, it made him feel better. With surprise, he realized it was almost a Mormon vision of heaven. Under normal circumstances, this would have amused him...but not this night.

Now, on a mountainside in Sonora, Mexico, surrounded by dark, with only the sounds of a few nocturnal animals and night birds to punctuate the quiet, the weight of the past few days caught up to him. It was hard being the strong patriarch in the face of such deep tragedy. He was tired of the burden. He gave in to what he'd been holding back. The ache overcame him, and he sobbed quietly.

+++

Well before sunrise, Bob had a cold breakfast of his leftover MRE from dinner. Even the coffee was cold, just instant, stirred into cold water. He told the others to eat something. It may be a long time until dinner. Before the sun was up, they were mounted and starting out. Bob's horse, Pepe, was picking his way along the trail in the predawn twilight. Bob was letting the horse worry about the trail while he concentrated on where he thought he'd seen a flicker of light the night before. There it was. He saw what he thought was light against the dark backdrop of the mountain.

He reined Pepe to a stop and pulled his binoculars from their case. He glassed the area where he'd seen the light. There he saw the fire. It was unmistakable. As he watched, he thought he might see movement, but it was still too dark and too far away to be sure. He called Luke up and handed him the binoculars. Luke had the best eyesight of anyone Bob knew. Pointing to where he'd seen the fire, he asked, "What do you see?"

Luke looked for a short time, turned to Bob, and said, "It's a campfire. I see movement, maybe only one person. Is that Grijalva?"

"I don't know. We're going to find out." Bob turned to see Pat close behind, listening intently. "You heard all that?"

"Yep, I heard, now what?"

"We're going to get there as fast as we can." Speaking to both, he said, "Stay with me. If any of your horses start to fade, swap to a mule." He secured his binoculars and clucked at Pepe, who immediately started moving down the trail at an easy lope.

They had reached the bottom of the canyon quickly, watered the stock and themselves in the stream, then started up the slope to the source of the firelight. Bob had given Pepe a tickle with his spurs to encourage him to move a little faster. They were making good time up the steep trail.

After climbing what Bob thought must be halfway up the slope, the horses were starting to blow pretty hard. He was considering slowing down or maybe even giving the horses a break and leading them for a while. As they climbed around a sharp, steep hairpin turn, there in the middle of the trail was a man. He was leading a string of burros loaded with beargrass. Both were surprised. Bob reached for his pistol, and the man raised his hands.

Bob reholstered his pistol and said, "It's OK. Manos abajo." "¿Mande?"

Pat spoke up. "Bob, I got this." Then Pat said to the man, "Pon las manos abajo."

The man lowered his hands. He still looked concerned and asked, "¿Que está pasando?"

In English, Pat repeated what the old man said. "What's going on?" Then he told the man not to worry. "No te preocupes."

They learned the campfire Bob had seen earlier was this man's. His name was Paco Ruiz. He was cutting beargrass and carrying it down the mountain to sell to broom manufacturers. He told them he had seen the Grijalva brothers the afternoon before, a few miles further on. He had been cutting beargrass a few hundred meters from the trail when he saw them. They were horseback with a couple of pack mules and three young girls who were on foot. He couldn't describe the girls except to say they all had dark hair and appeared to be young; he described them as niñas, not chicas.

Bob, with Pat translating, questioned Paco in detail. He had no idea where the Grijalva brothers were going. He said the horses and mules looked fresh enough, but the girls, who were tied to a rope, were being led by Pedro and looked tired. Diego was bringing up the rear, leading the mules. Paco addressed Bob, as the apparent leader of the Gringos, asking something about the niñas. Pat translated it as "Are you going to rescue the girls?"

"Si."

"Bueno," Paco answered. He then said in broken English, "Hermonos Grijalva very bad men. After get las niñas, kill los Grijalvas." He paused here to find the words, then, pointing to his ears, he said, "Escutche, no come back Bavispe. Go norte. Mas importante, no come Bavispe." Then he repeated it all to Pat in Spanish.

Pat looked at Bob to see if he understood. Bob nodded and said, "Get the girls, kill the Grijalva brothers, and escape north to the border."

Paco said, "Si, usted comprende."

Bob thanked Paco for his help. He considered asking him to contact Jorge, but decided against it. He felt sure Jorge would know of Paco's return and find out what he needed to know discreetly. Paco wished them luck and God's blessing, then started back down the mountain leading his string of beargrass-laden burros while the gringos headed up to find the Grijalva brothers and the three niñas.

With the information they'd received from Paco, Bob knew the girls were slowing down their quarry. He hoped to find them by tomorrow afternoon. Bob had slowed their pace; it was more moderate now. There was no need to push the horses to exhaustion. Besides, they now knew they'd need to ride all the way to the border, a straight-line distance of about sixty miles, which would be more like seventy or eighty miles in the mountains.

+++

They'd topped out on the ridge where Paco had camped, then descended into another canyon. In the canyon bottom, the trail turned uphill, paralleling the creek. While the trail was uphill, it was a very manageable grade. The three men were making good time when they came to the point where the trail forked, with the main trail breaking away from the stream and side-hilling up a long, steep slope to the south. According to the map, the trail would turn back to the east at the top of the ridge. They were only about a half mile from the Chihuahua line.

The tracks of their quarry had been plain to see since reaching the canyon bottom. Before that, on the slopes and ridge top where Paco had been cutting beargrass, his burros' tracks had wiped out the Grijalva party's tracks. Here at the fork in the trail, Bob was surprised by what he saw. He stepped down off his horse to have a closer look. "They're headed north," said Bob, pointing up the small trail that forked off to the northeast, staying in the canyon bottom. Then, pointing back up the other fork, the main trail, he said, "At least one horse and one mule, both shod, came down from up there. There are some burro tracks, too."

Pat and Luke joined him in inspecting the tracks. "They're fresh," said Pat.

Luke pointed to the ground, "Here's the girls' tracks." He squatted down to get a close look. He spread his hand over them, noticing how small they were. One of the girls was barefoot, one was wearing sandals without raised heels, and one was wearing tennis shoes. He knew Sandra had been wearing her tennis shoes. He touched her track. "It's her," he said. Bob and Pat left Luke to his pain, while they looked to see what else they could learn from the tracks.

What they found was that all the animals had gone north, up the canyon on the smaller trail. The Grijalva Brothers had been joined by another man who brought along at least one horse, one mule, and some burros. There were now three sets of adult boot tracks, one of which was accompanied by the imprint of a stick or cane. That would be Pedro Grijalva.

They had spent some time here. There were food wrappers, human feces, and paper scraps that had been used as toilet paper, lots of tracks disbursed over a broad area. There was a lot of equine feces. The grass was cropped, showing that livestock had been grazing. Bob said, "They camped here. Pat, are those tracks coming down the hill the same age as the Grijalvas'?"

Luke joined Pat in inspecting the tracks. After they looked over the tracks coming down the main trail as well as the ones starting up the small trail, they agreed. The tracks from the main trail were older, maybe yesterday, the same as the ones they'd been following up the canyon. The tracks up the small trail were very fresh. They were this morning's tacks. They could not find any tracks for the girls going up the small trail; it appeared they were riding, maybe on the burros.

"We're gaining on them," said Bob. With that, he checked his cinch and swung up into his saddle. Turning to the others, he said, "I've said this before, but I'm saying it again. You must follow my instructions, especially when we find them. I know you're both capable, but I need to reinforce the fact that I'm the only one here with experience against armed opponents."

"OK," they both answered.

CHAPTER TWELVE

Tres Cruces Ranch, Cochise County, Arizona, May 1996

Diane was in the kitchen brewing coffee and tea. Elaina, Pat, and Suzie's daughter were at the table with Ruth and Maria. They were working on obituaries for Suzie and Andy. A blue heeler was sitting by the table. The dog was alert with bright eyes and perked up ears. Pat had brought her to headquarters after the murders. She had been whelped at headquarters and spent the first year of her life here before going to Mountain Camp. She was as much at home here as she was at Mountain Camp.

Shoestring was a dog of impeccable lineage, being a descendant of Scooter, the finest elephant dog in Cochise County. She took her job of moving cattle and protecting all things to do with the ranch very seriously. Now she was more than a little upset. She sensed something was wrong, and she didn't like it. Pat was gone, she smelled Suzie's blood in the house, and the people, her people, were on edge. Her world was not right.

After serving the coffee and tea, Diane received a phone call. It was Bob's cousin, Scotty. He was giving her a heads-up that she would have a visitor within the hour. His name was Don. He was the commander of the Special Forces detachment that had arrived on the ranch the night before. She was surprised that the detachment had already been on the ranch for a day. Bob and the others had only just left two days ago. She'd spent enough time as an army wife to be impressed by such a fast response.

Shoestring stood, she sensed something, pricked up her ears, and rumbled a low growl, but nothing came of it, so after a while she sat back down, keeping an eye on the door. Soon, there was a knock on the door, sending Shoestring into a fit of barking as she rushed at the door with her hackles up and her teeth bared.

Diane waited for Elena and Joan to get Shoestring under control. While Elena held onto the dog, Ruth took a shotgun out of the wall rack and took up a position where she could cover the door, while Joan did the same with an old 35 Remington saddle gun. Maria remained seated at the table, watching the door. Once Diane was satisfied, she went to the door.

Standing on the porch was a young man, perhaps thirty years old. He was in full battle rattle, wearing olive drab fatigues of the old jungle fatigue pattern. Diane noted that there were no patches, no badges, nor markings of any kind on his uniform. She thought, 'This is no PX warrior.' When he saw Diane, he removed his patrol cap and asked, "Mrs. Hasett?"

"Yes."

"Hello, I'm Don." He waited for her response.

"Yes, of course. I just got a call from Scotty saying you'd be by. Please, come in. Then, turning to Ruth and Joan, Diane said, "It's OK." With that, Ruth and Joan lowered their weapons.

Don smiled at this and said, "It's good to see you're well prepared." He settled into the chair Diane offered him and accepted the offer of a cup of coffee while watching Shoestring warily. Diane noticed and said, "Don't worry about Shoestring. Now that we've accepted you, she'll treat you as one of her charges." Diane tried to joke. "You are now under the protection of Shoestring, or as she prefers to be called, the terror of all recalcitrant bovine critters, great scourge of coyotes, defender of the ranch, and descendant of the finest elephant dog in Cochise County." Diane caught a lump in her throat and said, "If only she'd been her that night."

"If only," said Joan, who stood up, excused herself, and left the room, trying to hold back the tears. Elana left to be with Joan to try and help.

Don asked, "Would that have mattered?"

"Yes, she'd have raised the alarm. Suzie would have had time to put up a spirited defense, as you professionals put it." This got Diane to thinking, and she said, "Which raises the question, how were you able to get to the door without her knowing?"

Don shrugged, "Just lucky." Then he got serious. "Your husband's cousin briefed me on what happened here. First, I want to offer my deepest condolences."

"Thank you," answered Diane.

He continued, "Officially, we're here for our annual desert training. Having said that, our concurrent mission this year is to patrol the area covered by and surrounding the Tres Cruces Ranch, focusing on detecting, locating, and deterring threats. You should not even notice our presence. We require no assistance from the ranch as we are fully supplied and have prearranged resupply points. He reached into his musette bag and removed a small radio. If you need to contact us in case of an emergency, use this. The frequency is set."

"Colonel Cooper will contact you by phone with daily updates if there are any. If you have any information for me, give it to him, and he'll pass it on. I encourage you to only use the radio in case of an immediate threat. Do you have any questions?"

Ruth asked a few questions about the operation of the radio. Don gave them a quick course on its use and how to set up the charger.

By this time, Joan and Elena had returned to the living room. "How long will you be here?" asked Joan.

"As long as it takes. We are prepared to stay up to a month. If it requires a presence for any longer, another detachment will relieve us. Desert and mountain operations are our focus, so this fits right in with our contingency preparation."

Don stood to leave. Diane shook his hand and thanked him. Joan and Elena did the same. Maria stood and offered her hand, saying, "It is good to have you here. We are grateful. I have asked Heavenly Father for protection from this evil, and he has sent you." She continued to hold his hand as a tear welled up in her eye."

Don was a little embarrassed by the sincerity of this old woman. "Mrs. Barnes, it is our pleasure to help."

Ruth followed him out the door and stopped him at the bottom of the steps, where she asked, "Don, isn't it?"

"Yes," he answered.

"Don what?"

He smiled, "I'm sorry, for now just Don. I hope that's OK."

"That's fine. We're having a rough time. With the continued threat here and our men off to God knows where trying to rescue Sandra, we can't just grieve the dead and missing. You being here removes one big source of worry. We're truly grateful."

"No thanks are necessary." Don paused a second then said, "I do have a question."

"Ask it."

"What's this about an elephant dog?"

It was an old joke. "Scooter, Shoestring's ancestor of twenty or more years ago was the finest elephant dog in Cochise County."

Don said, "But there are no Elephants in Cochise County."

Ruth smiled.

"Oh." He said. "I see. A formidable lineage indeed."

"Indeed." Sweeping her arm to indicate the landscape, she said, "This country requires formidable." On a more serious note, she said, "Please do not hesitate to ask if you or your troops, I mean friends, need anything. Are you aware of the houses and barns at Indian Springs, Mountain Camp, and Desert Camp?"

"Not really."

"If you have time, I'll show you on the map where they are and the location of good watering sources for spring and well water."

"OK, Doctor Hasett, is it?"

"Yes, you've done your homework, but Ruth is fine."

"OK, Dr. Ruth it is."

She wondered if he realized what he'd just said. Looking at his face, she saw a flash of recognition and embarrassment.

"Oh, I'm sorry. I meant nothing by that." He was trying to undo any insult he had caused.

"It's fine. No harm done." Ruth then spoke to her mother through the door and told her she and Don were going to Pops' office. She was going to go over the map with him.

Diane looked at Aunt Maria, who gave in to a slight nod. They remembered what it was to be a grown, but still young woman, attracted to a strong, confidant man. Ruth may be attracted to this young warrior, but she was no foolish youngster. Diane said, "Of course, Ruth, that's a good idea."

Diane decided she had better go out to the bunk house when the crew came in for supper. It was important that they at least know about the presence of the troops. She also decided it would be good to introduce the cowboys and Don to each other.

CHAPTER THIRTEEN

Sierra Madre, Northern Mexico, May 1996

In the mountains, Luna and Ivan were turned over to a man called Don Poncho. They changed from the truck to horses, and burros. Only Luna and her brother were left from the original group; they were joined by three other girls, not yet teenagers, but not still children.

The trip through the mountains was hard. The children rode burros, sitting on packsaddles with an extra pad on top. The sawbuck packsaddle had no seat or stirrups, and the tree bars could be pretty uncomfortable as they formed an open peak along the spine of the burro, not unlike the peak of a roof. It felt like riding astride a rail. As bad as it was, it was better than walking.

They'd been traveling like this for two days when they met up with another group. There were two men named Grijalva, leading three young girls. After spending a night together on the trail and traveling a couple of hours, the Grijalva brothers told Don Poncho there might be someone following them.

Don Poncho was concerned about this. He was already risking a lot by dealing with the Grijalva boys from Sonora without arranging it with El Chino or the Sinaloa cartel. If they were being followed by either side, it would end very badly, very quickly. Poncho pulled his knife and killed Ivan.

Pointing to the dead boy whose lifeblood was pumping into the dirt of the trail, Poncho said, "We leave him on the trail as a warning to whoever is following us." The Grijalvas protested the killing of the boy. It was a waste of money. Don Poncho responded coldly that it was a necessary warning; besides, it was no big loss, boys weren't worth much.

+++

Bob and the others had made pretty good time with the horses at a brisk walk. Pat and Luke had tried to get Bob to hurry and pick up the pace, but he'd insisted they not push the horses too hard. Finally, Bob got aggravated with their constant prodding to go faster. He stopped his horse, turned broadside blocking the trail, and said, "Look, I told you both that if you were coming with me, you had to do as I said, and you both agreed. Now you're bitching and whining like a couple of privates in the rear rank, or worse, *civilians*." Sarcastically, he added, "Let me ask you two hardened, man hunters, what are we trying to do here?"

"Get Sandra back," barked Luke. "We aren't that far behind. We can catch up with them soon if we hurry. The horses will last that long!"

"Wrong! It's to get Sandra back *home, alive!*" said Bob. There is an excellent chance that once we have her and the other kids, we'll be pursued by the assholes we're tracking or their partners. That means we must get back across the border and to the ranch. In order to do that, we have to stay away from any populated areas, including roads, until we cross the border. We can't go down to the flats and hitch a ride. We must stay in the mountains. How do we do that if our horses are used up?" Here Bob paused to let what he'd said sink in. "Do either of you really think we can cover sixty miles through these mountains on foot, with a bunch of kids in tow, while staying ahead of whoever might come after us?"

Luke kept pushing, "I disagree, we can move fast, get Sandra, and make it to the border before they know what's happened."

Bob was done discussing it. He had to regain control. There would be time to argue later, but now he needed quick obedience. Bob allowed himself a quick, inward, sarcastic grin and said quietly, "This is why civilians should stay home when shit hits the fan, no damn discipline."

Luke wasn't backing down. "You and Mom did it. You two crossed hundreds of miles of the toughest country on the planet with nothing."

Bob looked hard at his son. Rode his horse up too close, leaned forward into Luke's space, and looked his son in the eyes. There was no expression on Bob's face, and his eyes were drained of any emotion. "Yes, we did, we had no choice, and most importantly—we were both hard as nails, are you?"

Luke was surprised and hurt by his father's cold response. He leaned back and said, "Damn, Pops, that was harsh."

Bob straightened up, had his horse take a step back, and said, "Son, I don't mean to hurt you, but this is a nasty part of the real world that you've never had to deal with. If I need advice on wildlife, I'll ask you. If I need advice on cowboying, I'll ask Pat, but here, in this situation, I'm the experienced one. I'm the one with wounds, I'm the one with a body count. I'm the one who knows the tragic cost of letting emotions influence decisions. We will do it my way." Looking at them both, Bob asked using the familiar rather than formal, "¿Sabéis?"

They both looked a little taken aback. Sabéis was not how one addressed friends, family, or peers. It was how one addressed subordinates. Bob was not one to talk down to people, not his cowboys, not his soldiers, and certainly not his family, but he just had. This was a side of Bob they'd not seen before. They had pressed him too hard, and they knew it. They exchanged looks, nodded to one another, and answered that they understood.

"Bueno, now back to the task at hand." Pointing up the trail, Bob continued, "We're gaining on them. If we don't catch up with them before sunset, we'll get them in the morning. Then we'll head for the border.

"OK, boss," said Pat. "We're with you." Luke nodded his agreement.

They were climbing. They had passed above the mixed pinyon pine, juniper, and evergreen oak woodland into an environment dominated by ponderosa pine. The trail passed through a saddle between two peaks before descending into a shallow canyon. Bob halted the group in the saddle between the two peaks. They had been traveling about four hours from where they found the tracks, leaving the main fork and turning up the north fork of the trail. Pat and Luke loosened the cinches on their horses and raised the saddles to air out their horses' backs.

Bob quickly pulled his saddle off and handed his reins to Pat. He then found a rock to lean against, steadied his binoculars, and started glassing the canyon below. There was something on the trail. It wasn't moving. He focused and refocused his binoculars, but could not make it out. He called Luke over and asked him to have a look.

After a short time, Luke lowered the glasses and said, "It looks like someone's lying there."

"Any movement?"

"No."

Bob hurried back to where Pat was holding the horses. He threw his blanket and saddle back on his horse and said, "Follow me. Keep a distance of ten yards between you. It's downhill, so we're going to be gathering country pretty quick." By the time Bob finished saying this, he had tightened his cinch, secured the latigo with a buckaroo latch, swung up into his saddle, and had kicked his horse up into a lope. The others followed.

The ride down had some tight switchbacks, which the horses handled with a minimum of sliding and a few small washouts that were easily jumped. As Bob got close to the bottom of the canyon, he pulled his pistol. Then, just before rounding the last turn before the trail bottomed out, Bob reined his horse to a stop, dismounting in a hurry, he unholstered his pistol, moved to the bend in the trail, and looked around to see what was in the trail.

He waved his hand forward to motion the others up as he holstered his pistol and walked to the body. In the middle of the trail was a dead boy. He was young, perhaps twelve years old.

Bob squatted next to him. His throat had been cut. He'd been dead for a short time. The flies and ants were present, but the raven's crows and vultures hadn't found the body yet. Rigor had just started to set in, affecting his face and hands. Bob said, "He's only been dead for two or three hours." Removing a scrap of paper that was pinned to the boy's shirt with a note in Spanish, Bob handed it to Pat and said, "What does it say?"

"It says, don't follow or we'll kill you and your families."

"That's all?"

"Yeah, that's all."

Bob thought about this for a while. Then said to the others, "They don't know for sure that they're being followed. They killed that boy as a just-in-case. They may suspect they're being followed, but they're not sure. One thing is for sure, they don't know it's us."

"How do you know that?" asked Luke.

"If they knew it was us, they would have left Sandra for us to find. We'll have to keep on alert for a trap. Let's take care of this boy."

Luke didn't like this delay. "We can't take the time to bury him?" Bob snapped him a warning look. "OK, Pops, sorry."

They wrapped the boy's body in a rubber poncho and placed it beside the trail, piling rocks over the body. Bob took off his sweaty undershirt and laid it on the boy's grave. "Maybe the smell will keep scavengers away, at least for a little while." Turning to Pat, he handed him the notebook he always carried in his pocket, along with a pencil, and said, "Please leave a note. Say we found him on this day, only two or three hours after he was killed. We do not know his name. We have offered up prayers for his soul." Bob considered something and said to Pat, "Say it was the Grijalva brothers that killed him." The others looked at him. Bob shrugged his shoulders and said, "Fuck the Grijalva brothers. They've earned the notoriety."

They were near the top of the ridge that formed the north face of the canyon, where they'd found the boy's body. Before reaching the crest, Bob dismounted and told the others to do the same. Handing his reins to Pat, he said, "Luke, come with me. Pat, keep the horses and mules here. This shouldn't take long."

He removed his Mauser from where it was strapped in its scabbard on one of the pack mules. He kept his M16 cross-slung across his back. Luke pulled his 243 from his saddle scabbard. Bob chambered a round in the Mauser and flipped on the safety. He had a full magazine in the M16, and a round was chambered. "Let's go, stay behind me."

As they neared the top of the ridge, Bob asked Luke, "You remember what I told you about military crests?"

"Yes, I remember."

"OK, we're almost there. From here on, we crawl until we can get a good observation point."

Bob and Luke were settled in a nook behind a rock outcrop looking into a broad, shallow basin, perhaps a mile across. Luke was glassing the area with Bob's binoculars while Bob used the scope on his Mauser. Luke taped Bob on the arm and pointed. "Look, see where the trail disappears into the big pines about halfway across the basin?" asked Luke.

Bob took a while to find what Luke was referring to. "I think so. Is it by those two big hoodoos?"

"No, it's to the left of that, about three finger widths, and further away."

Bob continued to look through his scope and finally said, "OK, I've got it."

Luke said, "Follow the trail back towards us. You'll see it disappear behind a small rise."

"I've got it."

See where the trail reappears a little to the right and maybe a hundred yards closer to us?"

"Yes."

"Keep looking at that spot." Luke offered Bob the binoculars. "Here, Pops, you can see better with these."

"Damn, it's them." Bob continued to watch. "It looks like they're stopped for the day. I don't believe it. That's a ballsey bunch. They have a fire going. Either they have no idea we're here, or they're setting a trap."

"What do we do now?" asked Luke.

"We find out what we can." He handed the binoculars back to Luke and said, "Keep watching them. We think there are three of them plus the kids. Try and see if that's the case. If you can get a count on the kids, that would be good, and a count on the livestock would be useful."

"OK, Pops."

Bob looked at his son, "I know it's hard not to sneak over there and grab Sandra, but you must stay here. Once it gets dark, we will have the advantage."

Luke looked hopefully at Bob, "Do you really mean that?"

"Yep, we know where they are, who they are, and when to start the party. They don't know anything about us, and they have no idea if or even when there will be a fight. I'll be back soon." With that, Bob crawled back below the crest and returned to where Pat was holding the horses and mules.

"Pat, we've found them. Let's unsaddle these guys. We're not going to hobble them. We're putting up a picket line. I don't want any of them wandering off. We aren't making camp, we'll be busy tonight."

Bob explained to Pat what he and Luke had seen. They both had an MRE. Bob said they'd need the energy, then he led Pat back to Luke's look out. Once there, Bob handed Luke an MRE and asked, "Any news?"

"I counted three adults; I think they're all men. I see maybe six kids. I haven't seen any livestock."

"They must have them behind the rise, just beyond their camp. Do you see anything that looks like a fence line?"

"Yes, there's a fence line running from east to west. It disappears behind the rise, just like the trail, then picks up again and goes on down to the west."

"So, it crosses the trail behind the rise. There's a good chance there's a water point there, maybe a small corral. We've seen sign of cattle up here. Stay here and keep an eye on them. I'll be back in an hour or less."

With that, Bob unslung his M16, handing it to Pat, slipped down the slope a little way, and started at a trot to the east, keeping the ridge between him and his quarry as he climbed. Soon, he reached his goal. There was a tall hoodoo on the crest. He was now higher and closer by half a mile to what he suspected was the Grijalvas' camp. Using the scope on his Mauser he confirmed that the livestock was in a small corral that had a drinker. There was no windmill, so he assumed the water was piped in from a spring up the mountain.

From where Bob was, they could work around and get in behind the Grijalvas. It would be dark and slow going, but very doable. Bob slipped back down below the crest and returned to Luke and Pat.

+++

Bob was briefing Pat and Luke on what he had seen and what his plan was to free the children. All three men then jerked their heads towards the sound of three pops. Bob said, "Gunfire, let's go, follow me."

Bob stuck to the plan he had worked out in his head, with the exception that they were moving a lot faster and had started earlier than he'd expected. The moon, a waxing gibbous, had risen above the horizon and was providing plenty of light, allowing them to travel at a good pace without too many falls. It was still a long way to travel at night, and even with the moonlight, night played tricks on land navigation.

Bob estimated that they had covered most of the distance to the Grijalvas' camp, but he couldn't be sure. They had used the terrain to provide cover, but it also blocked their view of the camp and any landmarks they had used on the way up. He needed to find out exactly where the camp was. There was a slight rise ahead of them that might give him the view he needed.

Bob had Pat and Luke accompany him up the slope to have a look. When they neared the top, they dropped to their hands and knees and crawled the rest of the way. On the crest, Bob caught his breath and started scanning the area below. Luke patted Bob's shoulder and pointed at a gap between some trees. Bob couldn't believe his luck. There was the telltale glow that was visible for long distances at night. Some fool was smoking a cigarette in the open. He handed Luke his binoculars.

Luke glassed with the binoculars for several minutes, then whispered, "I see one man sitting. It looks like he's tending to something. He's smoking. I see what appears to be kids lying on the ground, but I can't be sure."

"Nothing else, no livestock?"

Luke glassed the area again. "I can't see anything else. I can't see the corral from here."

Bob slid back down the way they had come up until he was below the crest, the others followed. "Pat, I want you to go around to the right and find the corral. We need to secure any livestock that might be there. If any of the bad guys, try to get to the livestock stop them."

"How?"

"I don't care, just be sure it's not one of us."

"OK. Should I leave now?"

"In a minute." To Luke, he said, "You and I are going to crawl down the other side of this hill and get a better look at what's going on. We'll act on what we see. Pat, keep your eyes and ears open. Once we have the camp secured, Luke will give you three of his loud whistles."

Bob touched each of them on the shoulder, "You two ready?"

They both answered that they were.

"OK, let's go."

Bob and Luke were nearly to the bottom of the slope. Once they cleared the crest, they rose up and walked down the slope in a crouch, using trees and bushes as concealment. Now they stopped, scanning the area in front. Bob needed to know more about the camp. He was straining his eyes to see what was under the trees when Luke squeezed his arm. Bob could barely see Luke in the shadowed moonlight, but he could see that he was pointing at something. Luke removed his hand from Bob's arm and raised his rifle. Bob followed Luke's line of sight and saw it. A man was standing no more than thirty yards away.

Bob gently pushed Luke's rifle barrel down. He silently removed his knife from its sheath, handed Luke his rifle, and quietly approached the man. It felt as if it took an eternity to cover the short distance. As Bob neared the man, he saw that he was holding a rifle. The man was muttering to himself. Bob could not tell all of what he was saying, but he heard, mi hermano, and Pedro and cabrón Don Poncho. The man was crying quietly.

In one motion, Bob wrapped his left arm around the man's head, pulling it back as he plunged the knife into his neck, just under his right ear. As the man fell back, Bob wrenched the knife out through the front of his throat, thus ensuring there would be no cry for help. Quietly lowering the dead man to the ground, Bob squatted low, remaining still, listening for any sign of another potential adversary. There was none.

Bob stood up after wiping the blood from his knife on the dead man's clothes. Luke had joined Bob by this time. He whispered, "Pops, I can't see or hear anything except the kids. They're asleep or pretending to be."

"Let's check them out. Where was the guy you saw before?"

"Over by the kids."

"Lead on, I'll follow."

When Bob and Luke worked their way through a gap in the trees to an opening, they could see the kids lying on the ground and a man sitting, slumped over. Bob approached him, poked him with the barrel of his rifle, and watched as he toppled over dead with a cigarette butt in his mouth.

+++

Dawn was approaching in the Sierra Madre. After seeing to Sandra and the other kids, Bob had taken his time checking out the camp and the surrounding area. Once he was sure it was all clear, he had Luke whistle for Pat.

The dead man with the cigarette in his mouth had been killed by a bullet to the abdomen. He was still warm when Bob checked him. He must have died while smoking the cigarette. There was a cane next to him. Bob guessed he must be Pedro Grijalva. The man Bob had killed was likely his brother, Diego.

Pat showed up as Luke was gathering the kids and doing his best to comfort them. Luke was holding Sandra by the hand and fighting back tears of relief. His efforts to comfort the terrified children were not having much effect. Pat put his hand on Luke's shoulder. "I'll take care of this. You need to see to your daughter."

"Thank you, Pat."

"De nada, compadre."

With that, Luke walked away from the others and sat down, holding Sandra on his lap and sobbing. When Bob walked up, Sandra got up and ran to him. Bob gave his granddaughter a big hug. "How are you, kiddo?"

"I'm good. I was brave, Pops."

"Yes, you were. We'll get you home soon." Looking at Luke, Bob said to Sandra, "Go help your dad. He's been worried about you."

"OK, Pops. How is Andy? They hurt him. Is he OK?"

Bob looked at Luke, who shook his head, then he said to Sandra, "I don't know. We've been looking for you. We'll find out soon."

Pat gave Bob an accounting of the livestock in the corral. There were two horses, one mule, and four burros. There was one old riding saddle, five pack saddles, and lots of pads and saddle blankets. It looked like the kids had been riding the burros with pads over the pack saddles. Pat said there were two sets of horse tracks and one set of mule tracks following a cow trail to the west. There was something else; there was a dirt road leading downhill from the corral to the northwest. There were old vehicle tracks on the road, but nothing fresh."

The road was also unexpected and significant. It could mean trouble. Up until now, Bob had assumed the Grijalva brothers would be taking the kids off the mountains further north towards Sierra de Enmedio. This could well be a rendezvous point where they would be picked up and transported by vehicle. "You said the horse and mule tracks followed a trail, not the road."

"That's right, straight east."

"Damn," said Bob, pointing over towards the man he'd knifed. "I should have kept him alive for information." Pat looked at him with a hint of disbelief. Bob noted the look and added, "At least until I got what I needed."

"OK, we need to act fast and get these kids moving to the border. I'm afraid someone will be here looking for them. This could be a pickup point."

"Are we going to bury these two?" asked Pat.

"No, coyotes and ravens need to eat too."

Bob asked Luke to go back and get their horses and mules. He asked Pat to find out what he could from the children while he checked the two bodies for identification and took stock of what equipment and food were at the camp. He wanted to get packed up and, on the trail, as soon as Luke returned with their horses and mules.

Pat sat talking with the children. There were five in addition to Sandra. He learned and recorded their names, ages, and where they were from. They ranged in age from eight to twelve years old. They came from Sanora, Chihuahua, and Sinaloa. He also learned that the man who had joined them two days ago was Francisco Huerta. He preferred to be called Don Poncho. He had brought the older girl, Luna, and her brother, Gilberto. They said the older Girl, Luna, and her brother were from Durango. The children said the Grijalvas were mean, but that Don Poncho was worse. He had killed the boy to scare them. They didn't know where Don Poncho came from, but his accent sounded like Chihuahua. They were sure he was the boss.

The children told Pat that last night, Don Poncho got into an argument with the Grijalvas. He wanted to take the children straight to Janos. The brothers wanted to stay in the mountains and go to Sierra De Enmedio and contact El Chino from there. It seemed Don Poncho and given in, but when he started to leave with Luna, the brothers tried to stop him. That led to the shooting. Now the tracks leading to the east made sense.

"Was Don Poncho hurt in the shooting?" Pat asked.

The children didn't know; they were busy trying to hide.

After a meal of tortillas and beans, courtesy of the Grijalva brothers' supplies, Bob and Pat were packing up what food and bedding were left at the camp when Luke arrived with their livestock. Bob showed the two men the Sonoran, Mexico driver's licenses he'd found on the dead men's bodies. "It's confirmed. They were the Grijalva brothers. Suzie and Andy's killers have paid for their evil." Both Pat and Luke nodded in agreement, but neither looked consoled.

Bob said, "That finishes the revenge part of our job. It's never satisfying. It doesn't replace our loss, and it leaves a hole inside us, but it needed doing." He motioned towards Sandra and the children. "Now comes the most important part of the mission. Once they're across the border, we'll have accomplished something good. That should help. Let's get ready to go."

Luke went to organize the smaller children, while Bob and Pat, with the help of a couple of the older kids, packed the mules and saddled the burros. The two girls who helped them pack the mules were not pleased with Bob and Pat's work with the burros; they took over.

The girls padded the pack saddles and hung makeshift rope stirrups from the pack trees so they could be ridden with some comfort. This was a big improvement over sitting on the wooden wedge of a pack tree all day with your legs hanging down. Bob and Pat were impressed. They told the girls it was the first time they'd seen such a thing and asked where they learned it. The girls gave each other the look that children reserve for simpletons and said they grew up on farms, and everyone who wasn't stupid knew how to saddle a burro. Bob smiled and said, "I guess I'm just stupid." They thought that was probably the case.

In the growing dawn light, Bob could see that Sandra and Luke appeared to be in a serious discussion. He decided it was father-daughter business and chose to stay out of it.

As he turned back to the task at hand, Sandra ran over to him and said, "We have to find Luna."

Bob said, "Sweety, we need to get you and the other children back home."

She was not backing down. "Pops, we have to find her, please."

"Sandra, I need to get you back with your family. Your mother and grandmother are worried to death."

"Luna is family."

This set Bob back. "Luna has a family, and they want her home. What I will do is call a friend who can find her in Janos and take her home."

"She doesn't have a home. Her family's all dead. She needs a new home and a new family."

"But Sandra, you're my granddaughter. I have the responsibility to take care of you."

"She could be your granddaughter, too, just like me."

Bob was stumped. He thought about what she said. He hated the idea of this girl, Luna, being abducted and sold into a life of enforced servitude in a sweat shop, or worse, but he had a duty to Sandra, Luke, and Diane. Whatever decision he made, there was no time to dwell on it. They had to get the children to the border as quickly as possible. He decided she was right. "OK, I'll go and get her. Your father and Pat will take you home." Now he had to inform the other men.

When everything was almost ready, Bob said. "Pat, you're in charge of getting this bunch home, rely on Luke." Then, turning to Luke, he said. "Do all you can to support Pat." Taking a deep breath, Bob said. "Stay in the mountains until you get to Highway 2, avoid contact with anyone until you cross the border, and watch your back trail. Pat, you know where that chain link gate border crossing is in Animas Valley, right?"

"Yep."

"You should be able to cross there with no problem. When you get across the line, get word to Diane. There should be some

Diamond A or Cloverdale cowboys around that can get you to a
phone. Tell Diane to send someone to get you. Tell her to notify
Jane and Tommy; she knows who they are. Tell her I'll be in
touch. Got all that?" asked Bob.

"Yep. Where are you going?"

"To find Poncho and Luna."

Luke didn't like this. Looking at his father, he said, "I told
Sandra we couldn't go after her friend. Why are you doing this?"

"You know why. Sandra asked me to go get Luna, and I can't
deny my grandkids."

Luke knew there was no changing his father's mind. He was
a stubborn old son-of-a-bitch. "Pops, sometimes you really piss
me off."

Bob smiled at Luke and said, "Life's a bitch, son."

Bob looked at Pat and said, "I think you can make it to the
border in four or five days. Don't spare the stock, but don't put
yourselves afoot either."

Pat said, "You need to take a pack animal with you."

"No, I don't need much, I'll carry it."

"I can rig up something for you on one of these burros. You'll
need your bedroll and some food. We can double two of the kids
on a mule with a light load."

Looking at the road and tire tracks leading down the
mountains to the west, Bob said, "Alright, but let's hurry. We
can't spend any more time here. It's too busy."

Pat said, "We got it, Boss. We have plenty of animals to pack
supplies and still have enough burros and mules for the kids.
We'll be fine." Then he smiled for the first time in days and said,
"No hill for a climber, Boss."

"That's right, Compadre—no hill for a climber.

CHAPTER FOURTEEN

Sierra Madre, Chihuahua, Northern Mexico, June 1996

Bob had followed the trail of Poncho Huerta and Luna after leaving Luke, Pat, and the children. He had dropped the honorific, Don, in relation to Poncho Huerta. Their tracks had led to a pack trail they followed as it climbed the mountains to the northeast. The children had said Don Poncho wanted to get to Janos, where El Chino lived. Bob tried to imagine where Janos was in respect to his current location. All he could remember was that it was not far from the border, south of Sierra de Enmedio. When he reached the dip in the ridgeline where the trail crossed over, he stopped to rest his horse and burro and have a look at the country ahead of him.

After hobbling his animals on a bit of grass, he climbed a hoodoo. Once he was settled in, where his view was not blocked by ponderosa and Chihuahua pine, he scanned the area to the east. The mountains continued in one blue row after another before descending into the flat land with its numerous circular, green, irrigated farm fields that stood out from the semi-arid grassland and Chihuahua Desert scrub.

To the northeast, rising from the desert, was the unmistakable mass of Sierra de Enmedio. It had once meant temporary refuge for the Apaches when being pursued by the US Army. It had provided water, food, and rest before the next leg of their trek across the desert to the Sierra Madre. It looked to be thirty or more miles away. He figured this placed Janos to his east.

He estimated it to be about fifteen miles as the crow flies to the flat land due east of his location. If there was one thing Bob understood, it was that the shortest distance between two points was not necessarily a straight line in the mountains. It would more than likely require covering over twenty miles before he reached the flat land below.

Bob took up his binoculars and glassed the mountains ahead, looking for a sign of the trail or his quarry. He saw no sign of Luna or her captor, but that was no surprise. The mountains were heavily wooded with the typical mix of Madrian woodland vegetation. There were a few old aspens growing near the crest in old burn-scarred areas. They were being replaced by conifers like Douglas Fir and Ponderosa, and Chihuahua Pine.

Further down the slope were Juniper, Pinyon Pine, and a couple of species of evergreen oak. The slopes that didn't support trees were covered in a dense chaparral of Manzanita. Strung through this dark-shaded woodland were bright green riparian strands. Whose numerous small streams watered large stands of sycamore or cottonwood, ash, and walnut, with lots of willows filling in the gaps between the large trees and on the fringes. He lowered the binoculars and said, "Just like home."

Bob could follow the pack trail that Huerta and Luna were using, or he could try and get ahead of them. He continued to glass the country, hoping some option would make itself evident. Looking to the east, Bob made out some small villages below the mountains. Most were surrounded by irrigated fields. There was a large town much further away. It sat at the intersection of two major roads. Bob guessed that the road coming from the west and continuing to the east must be Highway 2. The other, he had no idea about, but it was headed south.

After extensive examination of the mountains to his east, he was unable to see any evidence of other trails. He could see no way to continue except to follow the pack trail. He'd have to be careful not to spook Huerta.

+++

It was two days since Bob had split up from Pat, Luke, and the children. He'd been careful to husband his animal's strength. The trail wasn't bad, but it was the mountains with its share of climbs and descents. Bob stopped frequently as he followed the trail to the east, checking the tracks in the trail, often walking to spare his horse the additional weight on steep climbs. He believed he was close to catching up with Huerta and Luna. He debated pushing harder. His horse and burro had plenty of bottom left; that was not the issue. He had to be careful he didn't stumble into Huerta, or worse, an ambush. It was important that when he made contact with Huerta and Luna, it was on his initiative.

The trail crossed another small stream above a small waterfall. The water tumbled down the boulder-strewn canyon below the ford, with one small waterfall after another. Bob let his horse and the burrow drink their fill. As he looked around, he could see that Huerta and Luna had stopped here. There were corn shucks from Tamales, the grass along the stream had been cropped by grazing livestock, but most telling was the manure left by the animals. It was still warm. They were closer than he thought.

There was a rock outcrop a short distance up the slope. Bob hobbled his horse and burro, and taking his Mauser, he climbed up the outcrop. Once on top, he had an unobstructed view.

There, five hundred yards ahead of him, he saw Huerta and Luna. The trail was descending gradually as it side-hilled along the spur, which descended as it continued to the northeast. It was apparent that the trail would cross over the spur not far from Huerta and Luna's location. Bob had a chance to catch them if he hurried.

As Bob started to climb down the backside of the outcrop away from Huerta's view, his burro began braying frantically. Bob stopped his descent, leaned out around the outcrop, and looked in the direction of Huerta and Luna. In a few seconds, they heard the braying. Huerta jerked a look back over his shoulder, scanning his back trail, then slapped Luna's horse with his reins and kicked his horse into a gallop behind her. Bob didn't think he'd been spotted.

Bob could see nothing through the trees as he climbed down, but the burro's braying had become more of a whimper. His horse was also squealing frantically. Bob jumped the last ten feet to the ground to see a mountain lion with its teeth firmly gripping his burro by the back of the neck. The burrow hadn't fallen over yet, but he was wobbling and about to go down. Bob had seated his Mauser in the pocket of his shoulder and fired a shot before he could think about it. The lion dropped dead off the burro's back from the headshot. The burro stood with his legs splayed wide, shaking violently. He soon gathered himself, pulled his legs underneath him, and gave the dead lion several kicks.

Bob approached his panicked livestock, speaking softly to try and settle them down. The horse's eyes were rolled back in terror, and he wanted nothing to do with Bob, but he wasn't going anywhere, as he'd managed to get himself all tied up with his get-down rope tangled in his hobbles. Bob decided to see to the burro first.

The burro, which Bob called Feo, looked as if he was going to take a bite out of the lion that lay dead at his feet. The lion was missing a sizable portion of his head and posed no threat to anyone. "Feo," said Bob gently. "It's OK, boy. Let's have a look." Bob avoided Feo's back end and kept a close eye on his front end. Stroking his flank and continuing to talk to the burro, Bob checked out his wounds. He had some deep puncture wounds on his neck and some scratches on his flanks. There was no blood coming from his nostrils or mouth. There was no arterial bleeding from the wounds. "You are one lucky jackass, Feo. You just might make it. Let's get this pack off of you."

Once Bob had seen to Feo, he untangled his horse and checked to see if he was sound. Everything with the horse was as it should be. Bob had to get moving. He decided it would be better to leave Feo on his own than to take him. The burro seemed to be all right, but Bob didn't think he was up to the fast pace that the current situation called for. Bob went through the pack saddle and removed two army blankets from his bedroll. He took out a couple of MREs, and some spare ammunition. He rolled it all up in the blankets and tied the roll behind his saddle. That would be all he'd carry on his horse.

He unhobbled the burro and said, "Feo, you're on your own. Stay away from lions." With that, Bob swung up into his saddle and put his horse up into a trot. He had to make up ground.

CHAPTER FIFTEEN

Chihuahua, Mexico, June 1996

Bob was close to catching up with Luna and Poncho. It was midafternoon of a cloudless June day. He was no longer in the mountains but in the desert. It was hot, he and his horse needed rest and water, but his quarry's tracks were fresh. He had to keep pressing. Then he saw it, a mile or less ahead, he saw their dust, then he saw them, two riders and a pack animal. He had them.

His horse was nearly done in, but they had to push hard. "Just a bit more caballo," he said as he spurred the horse up to a lope. Bob needed more from his horse than a casual lope, so he spurred harder but with little result. He had no choice but to pull a pigging string from his chaps and use it as a quirt. He began whipping his horse over and under in an effort to squeeze the last bit of speed from him. He felt bad. He knew he was demanding too much. The pace would result in the horse being ruined at best, or more likely dead, but Bob had to push him to save the girl. He said, "I'm sorry, caballo," as he continued to whip and spur.

The road dropped into a small draw where he lost sight of Poncho and Luna. Pulling his Mauser out of its scabbard, he pushed his horse up the far side of the draw, in a final effort to close the gap so he could at least have a decent shot at Poncho. What he saw when he had them in view emptied his tank. A stock truck was pulling away with horses and a mule loaded in the back. A man was standing on the passenger side running board with the door open. He waved at Bob, then crawled into the cab and closed the door as the truck drove away. Poncho had beaten him. Bob reined his horse to a stop. There was no reason to kill him while trying to run down a truck. Bob had lost; worse, Luna had lost.

+++

Bob was in the water lot where the truck had met up with Poncho and Luna. He stood next to his worn-out horse as he drank from a stock tank. He had removed the saddle to help his horse cool down. He had to get word back to his contact, Jane. He hoped he could call from one of the farms he'd seen from the mountainside. Since his horse was used up, he'd have to walk. He threw his blanket and saddle back onto his horse's back, and they started down the dirt road.

After walking for an hour, Bob came to a long driveway leading to a farmhouse. He didn't hesitate. He walked to the house, stood in the front yard, and called out. Soon, a middle-aged man walked out from behind the house. He was tall, blonde, and dressed in a long-sleeved chambray shirt with denim bib overalls and a straw hat.

"Buenas tardes," said Bob.

"Buenas tardes," answered the man.

Bob removed his hat and said, "Me llamo Roberto, mucho gusto." Then, struggling with his limited Spanish, he managed to get the message across that he would like to borrow the man's phone.

The man held out his hand, removed his hat, and smiling answered in English, "My name is Eli Reimer, it's nice to meet you. You are in luck, my wife and I are fairly liberal, we have a phone, so yes, you can make a call."

Bob was relieved. He'd expended his limited Spanish just to get to this point. "Oh, thank you, Sir. I can pay for the use of your phone."

"That will not be necessary, Roberto. I can see you are in need." Eli pointed to Bob's horse. "As is your horse. Let us get him some feed. After he is seen to, we will go in and get you some food and the phone."

"Thank you, Eli. That is most kind."

When Eli took Bob into his house, he introduced his wife, Anna. She offered Bob a chair at the table and brought him a glass of milk and a plate of sliced cheese. Bob had heard of Mennonite Cheese or Queso Menonita, as it was called in Mexico. It was a semi-firm cheese, light yellow, almost white in color, and tasted similar to cheddar. Bob was glad of the change from MREs

Bob was enjoying his cheese and milk, Anna spoke to her husband in a language that sounded like German, but somehow it was different. He turned to Bob and told him supper would be ready in half an hour. "Would you like to make your call now?"

"Yes, please."

On the phone, Bob had passed on the information about the Grijalvas and the children to Jane. He told her to ask Gomez of the Border Patrol for the location of the old Diamond A crossing west of San Luis Pass. That's where she would find Pat, Luke, Sandra, and the other children. They would be there soon, probably in one to three days. She said she'd have someone meet them at the border and get them back to the ranch. The children would be turned over to the Border Patrol. She would contact the Mexican Consulate in Tucson and notify them.

Bob thanked her and then said, "I have more. I'm going after Francisco Huerta and a girl he's holding captive named Luna. I think they're headed to Janos to hook up with El Chino."

She paused before saying anything. This was not part of the arrangement. He was to recover his granddaughter and avoid unnecessary contact that would risk exposure. He wasn't there to do battle with the cartel-driven human trafficking industry. He had accomplished his mission. "That's out of scope."

"I know, but this girl did all she could to protect these kids, and she paid the price. We can't abandon her, and Huerta needs to be stopped."

"What happens after that? Do you go after the next level up the ladder, and then the next, and so on until they catch you, skin you alive, and hang your body from a bridge for newspaper copy? I can't have you running loose down there. You have no official status. I can't protect you. Besides, your family needs you here."

"Once I find Luna, I'll be done."

"Do I have your word on that?"

"Yes, you do."

Jane took a deep breath and decided to bite the bullet. "What do you need?"

"I'm about thirty miles west of Janos. I need a contact there."

"I can send someone to pick you up and take you to Janos," she offered.

"No, not yet. I'm afraid someone coming to get me might be noticed as outside activity." Bob was on a Mennonite farm, and the Mennonites had a reputation for keeping to themselves. He did not want to attract any attention to Eli and Anna. "I think I can get there without drawing any attention. If not, I'll be in touch."

She said, "I'll pass this on and set the meet." Then she switched to the CEOI code sheet and sent him the location, date, time, and the introduction phrase and response for his contact.

Bob thanked her and asked her to let Diane know what was happening. She said, "Diane is my next call. Good luck, and don't make me regret this."

Bob debated how much to tell Eli. Finally, he decided he could trust him with the basics that he was in pursuit of a human trafficker and his captive, but no more.

After hearing what Bob had to tell him, Eli said, "I must go to town tomorrow. I have business to conduct. I can hook up the trailer and give you and your horse a ride."

"I appreciate that, but won't it be noticed that you're with an outsider?"

Eli laughed. "We are seen with outsiders on occasion."

"Alright, that would be a big help. We don't need to worry about the horse, though. He's in need of a long rest, and he's of no use to me in town. You should keep him."

"I can't do that," Eli said this in such a way as to leave Bob with no doubt that he would not accept the horse. "I can keep him until you come to get him or send for him."

"Thank you, Eli. That's very generous."

"Anna has made up the spare room for you. There is a towel and some clean clothes on the bed. Anna will draw your bath. Leave your dirty clothes on the floor of the bath. Anna will wash them and have them ready for tomorrow. We will leave in the morning, early. Goodnight, Bob." With that, Eli left.

After a big breakfast, Bob and Eli had loaded the truck and were now pulling out of the farm. The sun had been up for about an hour. Eli explained that it would be a drive of less than two hours to get to Janos

+++

Luna Ortiz was chained to a pipe in a small shed behind the main house at Rancho de Nuestra Señora de Guadalupe. Such a pious name was meant to cover the real purpose of this remote property at the foot of the Sierra Madre Occidental.

The pipe she was chained to was about waist high, running horizontally along the walls on three sides of the shed. On the pipe were several chains hanging from steel rings, almost like oversized curtain rings. At the end of each chain was a pair of handcuffs. The rings could slide along the pipe between the brackets that held the pipe to the wall, allowing some movement along the wall. In each of the corners were two buckets, one that served as a latrine and one with water and a dipper that was for washing and drinking. On the floor were some old, filthy reed mats and a few moth-eaten blankets that served as sleeping pallets. There was nothing else. Luna was alone in the shed.

She was tired, scared, and hungry. In a month, she had lost her family to violent murder, and her virginity to brutal men. Now she was chained up in a filthy shed. She was sure that whatever was in store for her was bad. All she wanted to do was go back to a time when she was happy at home with her family, planning for her celebration to Quinceañera.

Now there can't be Quinceañera, I'm not a girl passing into womanhood. My father is dead; if he were alive, he could not present a soiled daughter to suitors. I'm spoiled. I'm ruined. I am shamed, and all my family are dead. She thought she had no tears left; she was wrong. She sobbed and mourned the loss of her future.

Don Poncho opened the door to the shed. Luna shaded her eyes from the bright light of the afternoon sun that flooded the otherwise dark shed. Don Poncho entered and approached Luna. She recoiled instinctually. "Don't be afraid, Mija. I'm your friend and protector. I'm not letting anybody hurt you. Here's your lunch." He bent over to kiss her on the head. Then left.

Now alone in the shed, Luna was shaking. She hated it when he called her Mija. She hated it when he touched her. She was no daughter to him, nor was she a sweetheart to him. She hated him. He treated her as badly as the others had. There were no more gangrapes, but that was because he kept her for himself. He took her every night.

With a final shudder, Luna regained control of herself. Don Poncho had left a tin plate of beans with some hot tortillas folded and wrapped in foil, and a can of Coke. She was famished; she ate every bit of her lunch, wiping the plate clean with her last tortilla, and she wished for more.

She tried to make sense of what had happened to her. She had tried to be good and live up to the priests' teaching. She tried to save her brother, but he was dead. She had tried to protect the younger children, but they were gone, and maybe they were dead too. The saints had not answered her prayers. They had abandoned her. All she got was more beatings and worse; sweaty, dirty, men on top of her, behind her, or standing over her, all the time forcing their members into whatever openings they chose. Were the priests wrong? Did God's love not rule the world? Did evil rule the world?

This weighed heavily on the young woman. Survival was now her primary concern. No, it was more than that; it was her only concern. Life had become a struggle just to see the next day. It was getting harder. She didn't know how much more she could take. Maybe if she pretended to like Don Poncho, he'd give her more food. That thought made her feel sick, but she was hungry.

CHAPTER SIXTEEN

Janos, Chihuahua, Mexico, June 1996

Bob was sitting on a park bench in the shade of some large trees. The tree trunks were painted with a protective coating of white paint up to five or six feet above the ground. Their shade was important on this afternoon of nearly one hundred degree heat. He had been told by Jane to sit on a bench near the gazebo. His contact would be there between three pm and four pm. He'd been sitting on the bench and thumbing through a newspaper for a couple of hours.

When he arrived at the park three hours early, he'd gone to a shop where he bought a nice shirt, jeans, and a small duffle, looking less like a worn cow puncher and more like a tourist. He spent his first hour wandering around, getting his bearings. It was a unique Plaza; aside from the trimmed lawn, neat tree-lined paths, and the ubiquitous gazebo common to most of the plazas he'd seen, this one had a large, covered area in one corner that served as a basketball court, and apparently a band stand as it also had a stage at one end.

At the scheduled time, a woman of perhaps forty approached and sat next to Bob. She was tall with a slender, but not skinny, figure. Her face was attractive with a hint of sternness. Her complexion was flawless. She had hazel eyes and light brown hair. She looked at him and asked, "Are you here for el baile?"

Bob folded his newspaper and answered, "No, I can't dance."

The woman slid closer. As she took his hand, she said, "We're a couple." Under her breath, she continued, "My name is Margarite Terrazas, I know your name."

"Are we married?"

She assumed a coquettish air about her, leaned over, and gave him a kiss. "No, we're having an illicit affair. You're my married American land baron, John Johnson. You have come down to look over some horses I have for sale." Then she added with a smile, "and some recreation. Do you know anything about horses?"

"I know which end to hang the feed bag on." He joked. "Yes, I know a little."

"Good," she said. "Now come with me."

She led the way to her car, a new Mercedes G-Class. As they approached, Bob said, "Nice car."

"I like it," she said as Bob held the door for her.

She carried herself with elegance. Her clothing was expensive and fashionable beyond what one would expect for an afternoon stroll in the park. Her carriage was dignified, and her speech and mannerisms bespoke money and confidence. This was a woman of substance.

They did not speak about why Bob was really in Mexico until they were driving. After she pulled away from the curb, she turned on the radio and said, "Tell me what you can. I was given only cursory information."

Bob filled her in on everything. She questioned him thoroughly until she was convinced she had all the information she needed. "Don't trust anyone here. The cartels are in everyone's pockets. The Police, the army, prosecutors, and judges are all on the cartels' payrolls. What's worse, the cartels are at war with each other for control, so you can't tell who's who, or who's in charge."

"Understood," said Bob.

"We are staying at one of my family's old estancias not far from town. We will have to play this cover of lovers, even to the point of sharing a bedroom. I hope you don't mind the floor. The servants are good and loyal for the most part, but I can't pay them enough to ensure their silence, so ... you understand."

"Yes, I understand. The floor is fine."

"The house may be bugged, so we will have to talk outside."

Bob had spent most of his army career gathering and analyzing intelligence across the globe. He was no rookie to clandestine activity. He'd used skullduggery to gather and analyze information on enemy targets while working counter-narcotics. He was OK with sneaking around the mountains of Peru hunting for a drug lord, who was terminated with extreme prejudice. It was all part of the game that he was familiar with and comfortable with, but this level of intrigue and clandestine activity was new to him. He was not sure he could pull off openly playing the part of someone else. It made him uneasy.

That evening, Bob and Margarite were sitting outside after they'd finished dinner. The sun had gone down below the mountains to the west, and the temperature had dropped enough that Margarite had draped a rebozo over her shoulders. They were both sipping wine while Bob was smoking a Cuban cigar, which she brought out to him. After a time, Margarite broke the silence. "There is no sign of Huerta in Janos. We've been watching El Chino since yesterday, so far, nothing. Could you have missed Huerta and Luna?"

"I know I was on them until yesterday when they loaded into the stock truck. After that, I know nothing."

Margarite didn't say anything for a while, then said. "Bob, we may have to go get El Chino."

Bob was surprised. "He's a big wheel, isn't he?"

"Yes, he is. It won't be easy."

"Are you sure about this?"

Margarite looked at Bob and answered, "No, I'm not sure. I don't like it. This struggle between the cartels has everything in turmoil. Anarchy is the order of the day; it is unmanageable. My links are broken. My sources have dried up or disappeared. What's true today is not true tomorrow. I would rather wait until the dust settles and see who winds up on top. Then we could get back to business as usual, but for some reason I'm not aware of, recovering this child and catching Huerta have become some sort of priority." She paused with her arms folded across her chest, looked up at the stars, took in a deep breath, and released it in a dejected sigh. She looked at Bob and said, "If we are to do this, we need information, and as far as I know, only El Chino has any."

Bob was curious to know more about this woman. Why was she doing any of this? She obviously didn't need the job. She was Mexican and putting herself at serious risk by acting as an American asset. "Margarite, this is risky business. May I ask why you're doing this?"

With an irritated tone, she asked. "Doing what, helping you find the girl?"

"Well, yes, that and the rest, working for the company."

"I may have been born and educated in the US, and I do have family on both sides of the border, but I am Mexican. I am a Terrazas. My family has been in Chihuahua forever. We are leaders in Chihuahua. Do you understand what that means?"

"I think so."

"Now, these people, these animals, are ruining my country. They're destroying everything that is good about Mexico. I work with the US because its agencies haven't been bought yet. They are my best hope of resisting the cartels, of fighting back against these animals, of trying to stop or at least slow down the rot in Mexico."

Bob took a deep breath, smiled at Margarite, and said, "Well damn, we're going to snatch up a cartel capo." Raising his glass, he said, "No guts, no glory."

With a tone of disdain, she said, "You're one of those, aren't you?"

Bob sensed danger. "One of who?"

"One of those innocents who believes there is a simple right and wrong." Looking hard at him, she said. "I imagine you've tilted at a few windmills in your time." She paused, took a couple of deep breaths, and said in a voice that betrayed her frustration, "How naïve, how American, how incredibly cowboy." She raised her glass and, with her best fake smile, said, "Salud."

CHAPTER SEVENTEEN

Sierra Madre, Chihuahua, Mexico, June 1996

Pat and Luke were glassing their back trail. The day before, Pat had spotted a group of horsemen following them. Since then, He, Luke, and the girls had pushed hard, not even stopping for the night. The nearly full moon made it possible to cover some very rough ground at night. Pushing so hard through rough terrain and in the dark was not without danger. It cost them a mule lost to a broken leg and a burro killed when she tumbled into a deep canyon. Pat and Luke's horses had played out. They were now mounted on the last two remaining horses, but most importantly, all the children had made it.

After four days of rough travel, the border was only a few miles away. The children had been champs, riding when they could, walking when they must. Now that they were so close and had the advantage of an easy trail to the border, Pat and Luke stripped the remaining burros and mules of packs, mounted all the children, and sent them ahead. Pointing at a large mountain on the northern horizon, Pat told them, "Keep that peak between your animals' ears. No matter what happens, go north, help will be there." Then he slapped one of the mules on the butt and said, "Aora, vosotros vais rapido." Now, go quickly.

If there was to be trouble, the men didn't want the children caught up in it. Pat and Luke would stay behind to hold up any pursuers long enough for the kids to get across the border.

What Pat and Luke didn't know was that less than four miles to their north, Don and his detachment were watching. One of the team, looking through high-powered optics, said, "I've got them, or at least the kids. They're coming this way, about three miles out. They're riding horses, no wait—and donkeys."

"Smitty, are there any others?"

"Not with them." Then they heard distant gunshots. Smitty moved his field of view beyond the children. "I'm scanning. I can't make out anything, it's too far."

Standing next to Don was Rodriguez, who asked, "Now?"

"Roger Rod, go get the kids." Then, turning to his number two man, Don said, "Chief, have your people ready to put down supporting fire."

"Roger."

Rod and his men were already through the border fence and running towards the children when Don raised Jane on the satellite phone and said, "Operation Pied Piper is underway, out."

The distant gunfire increased in volume and was joined by more gunfire coming from closer. "What's going on?" asked Don.

Smitty, who was peering through the optics, said, "I've got 'em, southwest fifteen hundred meters. I can mark the target for Chief."

Don answered immediately. "Do it."

With that, the report of a .50 caliber round boomed across the desert. The tracer hit the ground among a pile of rocks nearly a mile out. Chief's men immediately put a heavy concentration of accurate machine gun and mortar fire on the target. After a minute or less, Chief called, "Cease Fire." The shooting from the rock pile had stopped. "Don, I'd like to put a little heat on that rock pile from time to time to remind them to keep their heads down."

"Roger, Chief. Keep 'em quiet."

Rod came up on the coms and said, "I need to clear that rock pile. It poses a threat to the kids. I'm taking Pahoa and Jones with me to clear it, and I'm sending Jackson with Arceneaux and DeLuca to get the kids."

"Roger," answered Don.

As Rod and his men were clearing the rock pile, Smitty was scanning the area where he thought the earlier shots had come from. Then he saw them. There were two men who looked like civilians, engaged with someone to their south. These must be the men bringing the children across the border. "Don, I have two men and two horses on that low rise. It appears they're firing to the south. They could be the rescuers."

At the same time as this conversation was going on, Jackson's team was rushing to collect the children. The children were riding as fast as their tired mounts could cover ground, and the soldiers were running towards them as fast as they could. The mile between them was closing fast.

Don saw it first. A dust cloud to the east, where three pickup trucks were coming down a dirt road. They were moving fast. It looked like they planned to cut off the Children's escape route. Smitty had also picked up the movement and was glassing the trucks. He told Don they wore no military or police markings, but they had pedestal-mounted weapons, probably machine guns. There were several armed men in each truck. Soon, they began to fire at Ryan's location and at Jackson's men who were rushing to the children.

Their shooting was inaccurate, causing no real threat to Don and those with him, but the trucks were closing fast with the children. Rodríguezes had secured the rock pile and was now doing what he could to slow the trucks, but at a distance of nearly a mile from his position, small arms fire was not very effective.

Calmly, Don said while pointing at the trucks, "Chief."

"Rodger."

The M240 machine gun and the 60mm mortar took the trucks under fire, as did Smittie's .50 caliber rifle. It only took a few bursts of machine gun fire, three mortar rounds, and a scattering of .50 caliber rounds to reduce the number of trucks to one and send that one packing back to the east, swerving nearly out of control on its blown-out tires.

It was now that Pat and Luke decided to mount up and ride hard for the border. They had been keeping an eye on what was happening with the children and could only imagine that the troops were friendly. It was clear that the children would be safe.

As Luke and Pat were riding hard for the border, Jackson's team reached the children. The soldiers smiled at them and waved them on towards the border, shouting encouragement in both Spanish and English. Falling in beside the children, the soldiers double-timed to keep up with the trotting mules and burros. Rodrigues's team soon joined them and fell in behind, forming a rear guard. The border was only a mile away.

When Don called Jane and reported that Operation Pied Piper was underway, it had set a whole string of actions in motion. First, the Border Patrol was alerted to send its pre-staged van and a truck with a stock trailer to the border crossing for the children and their livestock. A Night Stocker Chinook was alerted to pick up Don and his team. Tommy Juddson was notified that Sandra, Luke, and Pat were on the way in, and finally, word was passed to Margarite Terrazas in Janos.

The children and their rescuers were all on the US side of the border. Only Luke and Pat had to get across. They were riding as hard as they could on their tired horses. They were half a mile from the fence when bullets snapped over their heads. Looking back over his shoulder, Pat saw muzzle flashes coming from one of the destroyed trucks. Suddenly, the fence line in front of him lit up with return fire. There were no more shots from behind, but he felt a burning in his thigh as his horse fell.

Luke reined to a stop, leapt from his horse, and seeing that Pat's horse was finished, he lifted Pat into his own saddle. Then, leading his horse at a trot, he started the last half mile to the border. By the time he'd covered a couple of hundred yards, he was surrounded by members of Don's team. They took over, leading the horse, and started treating Pat's wound while he was still in the saddle.

As they crossed the border, Sandra rushed to her father and jumped into his arms. "Daddy, are we safe now?"

"Yes." With Sandra clinging to him, Luke walked over to where the medic was dressing Pat's wound and starting an IV. "Pat, we did it. We got all of them across."

"Yes, we did." Pat smiled and added, "Now we can tell your old man we've met the elephant."

"Damn right, but I don't want to do it again," said Luke.

"Me neither, amigo." A look of sadness crossed over Pat's face. "Suzie would be so proud of what we did."

Luke didn't know what to say. Pat had lost his wife, and he had lost his son. He said what he thought would help. "She knows. She's proud of you."

Pat looked at Luke. His Gray eyes welled up with tears, and he said, "Andy would be proud of his father. Andy *is* proud of his father."

Despite their accomplishment in bringing the children to safety, the two men were overwhelmed by their loss. Now that they were safe across the border, the grief set in. Luke said to Pat, "I think Suzie's babysitting Andy."

Pat smiled, "Yes—I like that."

Don walked over to Pat and Luke and introduced himself. Then he asked the medic how Pat's leg was. The medic told him the bone was intact, and no arteries had been hit; blood loss was not bad, his vitals were pretty good considering, and there was no sign of severe shock. He was ready to travel.

With a slightly wounded civilian in tow from the rock pile, Rodriguez approached Don and asked, "What about him?"

"Find out who he is, who he works for, why they were after the children, anything along those lines. Then release him."

"Roger."

CHAPTER EIGHTEEN

Janos, Chihuahua, Mexico, June 1996

Bob was relieved to know Sandra, Luke, and Pat were safe. Jane's call had come as he and Margarite were preparing to implement their plan. Now he could concentrate on Luna without distraction. The plan was simple. El Chino's cover was a legitimate import export business. He ran it from a small curio shop filled with cheap souvenirs. Bob would go into el Chino's store, ask some innocent questions. The sort of thing a dumb gringo tourist in search of a good time might ask. While this was going on, two of Margarite's operatives would come in through the back entrance, sedate El Chino, and load him into the car that was waiting out back. Bob would simply leave through the front door with some gaudy souvenirs as if nothing untoward had happened. Margarite would pick him up a few blocks away. That was the plan.

Bob walked into the shop and started looking around at the trinkets. Eventually, a young man, actually a teenage boy, came into the shop from the back room, posing as the shopkeeper. This was not El Chino. Bob continued to poke around and attempted to engage the boy in conversation. He was very nervous and distracted. While Bob tried his best not to alarm the boy, Margarite's operatives came in from the back, seized the young man, locked the front door, and motioned Bob to follow them into the back room. There was El Chino on the floor. He'd died hard. Whoever killed him meant it as a message. Bob left to meet with Margarite as planned while the operators loaded the boy in their car and headed to their pre-arranged destination. They would contact Margarite after questioning the boy.

Margarite put a CD in her player and turned up the volume to mask any conversation she and Bob were to have. "What happened?" she asked.

"I don't know except that El Chino's dead. His body was in the back room. He'd been dead for several hours. Your men grabbed a boy who was there. They said they were going to interrogate him and get back to you."

Margarite considered this for a while, then asked. "Can you tell me anymore?"

"He was tortured. We didn't spend any time checking over his body, but he'd been beaten and burned."

"Do you have any idea who the boy is?"

"No, all I know is he was armed and nervous."

"Well, we'll know soon enough. He'll talk."

"What now?" Bob asked.

"It looks like it's time for our fallback plan."

Bob looked at her and asked, "Is there a fallback plan?"

Margarite shook her head in exasperation. "What do you think? Of course, there's no fallback plan. This operation is purely reactive. There was no prior planning at all. Everything about it is spur of the moment; it's amateur hour."

Bob was getting a little irritated with Margarite's attitude. He said, "Welcome to the tactical world. There is never enough of anything, especially time and intel assets. The unexpected is the order of the day. Everything is fluid. Actionable items are perishable. By necessity, tactical intel is often quick and dirty."

Margarite's response was derisive. "Quick and dirty, what can be good about that?"

"It's timely. If intelligence is late, it's no longer intelligence; it's history. It may lack precision, but it is accurate enough to meet the needs."

"Now what?" she asked.

"Now you and I are going to come up with a plan. If and when things change, we'll readjust." Here Bob paused for emphasis and said, "As often as necessary."

Margarite knew she had pushed her case far enough. "OK, we will play it your way."

"First, we need intel. Other than the boy, are there any other sources?"

"Not until we hear from my men. Hopefully, what they learn will give us some ideas."

"Margarite, I can't pretend to know how to do your job. I'm not trying to how to do it. I'm sorry."

She smiled, "I know, it's OK. This frenetic pace is out of my comfort zone. We'll adjust to 'quick and dirty.'"

In the afternoon, while they waited to hear from Margarite's operatives, she received a call. It was the second call from Jane. She had already passed on the information that Luke, Pat, and the kids were safe. This call was about Rodriguez's interrogation of the civilian. It had uncovered some surprising information. Someone told Jarez that the Grijalva brothers were going rogue. They planned to bypass the cartel and move traffic across the border into New Mexico. Jarez had sent out sicarios to eliminate the Grijalvas and take possession of their captives. It was rumored that El Chino was suspected of duplicity.

+++

Margarite returned from the phone call with her men. The boy said he would be in deep trouble. The bosses would think he betrayed them. He was as good as dead. He wanted protection from reprisal. Once he was offered that he would talk. Margarite told them to agree to his request. She and Bob would be there soon.

Margarite was driving a Chevy Cheyenne pickup truck. The model was popular and commonplace in Mexico. They were headed to the old, disused hay barn on the north end of Margarite's ranch. "Bob, we're going to make a blustery entrance. We want noisy and scary."

"Sounds like a plan."

As they pulled up to the gate, one of Margarite's operatives came out and met them. She filled him in on her plans and told him to alert the other operative. They were to act surprised and concerned by her arrival. Once Margarite figured enough time had passed for the message to be passed, she pushed down hard on the accelerator and raced into the yard, then slid to a stop in a choking cloud of dust. She and Bob exited the truck and burst through the door. They acted enraged and began shouting at the operatives in English and Spanish as they motioned angrily at the boy. It was all a show to frighten him.

The boy was scared and explained he was supposed to mind the shop as if everything was OK until someone came to recover El Chino's body, but he said the gringo and these two men kidnapped him. Marguerite prompted him to tell her more. Reluctantly, he continued.

There were two sicarios from Juárez and three Gringos. They knew El Chino had a ranch where he staged people before shipping them across the border. They wanted to know where it was and tortured him to find out.

Margarite asked, "What did he tell them? Where is it?"

"He didn't say. He died."

Under intense pressure from Margarite, he claimed he knew nothing more. She didn't believe him.

"He's holding back. I have an idea. I want to shock this boy into a higher level of fear. He needs to be terrified. I have an idea." She explained what she wanted.

Bob asked, "OK, who's going to be Hannibal Lecter?"

"You are." She said.

Bob asked, "Who are you going to be?"

"As always, I'm your handler."

"Funny."

Margarite smiled and said, "I thought so."

This conversation was all in English and intentionally with raised voices. Bob's voice and mannerisms were becoming agitated.

When they thought they had elevated the tension in the room to the proper level, Bob turned and rushed the boy who was tied to a chair. Bob rammed into the chair, knocking it over. He pulled the boy's pants down, pulled out his stock knife, and grabbed the boy's scrotum. Margarite, continuing the charade, grabbed Bob and tried to pull him off the boy, shouting in English to stop.

Bob relented and, in his best gringo Spanglish, while waving the knife in the boy's face, he said, "OK, you son of a puta, today you have mucho suerte. La Señora, saved you, for now." Then, looking at the boy's crotch, Bob smiled. And sliced his knife through the air, making a snick sound, saying, "Maybe later l have your juevos for comida."

The boy was duly terrified. He was confused. He had thought he was dealing with a rival cartel or corrupt local government officials, but who was this gringo. Was he an American drug police? After Kiki Camarena was kidnapped and killed by the crazies from Sinaloa, the gringos got mad and started making trouble for the cartels. Some said they were very dangerous. Everyone knew gringos were evil.

The boy began speaking to Margarite in Spanish. He felt that this woman, who had stopped the gringo from taking his testicles, was his chance to live. She questioned him briefly, but he balked at answering her questions. He just begged for mercy. She got a sad look on her face, gave a deep sigh, stood, and started to walk away. She motioned to Bob, waving towards the boy, and said, "He's yours."

As Bob pulled the knife again, the boy cried out, "No, no por favor!" He pissed himself and shouted. "Te lo contraré todo." Margarite motioned for Bob to stop. She had the boy; now he would talk.

The boy didn't know much, but he had heard some talk about a Ranch used by El Chino. He thought it was called Nuestra Señora. It was a place of Brujaria negro. It was evil. Everybody knew El Chino was a brujo.

Nuestra Señora was the name the boy gave for the ranch used by El Chino. Margarite knew of no ranch by that name, but there was a ranch known as Rancho de Nuestra Señora de Guadalupe, named for the Virgin Mary of Guadalupe. There were rumors that it was a place of black magic. She explained all this to Bob.

The irony was not lost on him. "So, the Ranch of Our Lady of Guadalupe is being used to traffic girls. That's some cynical shit." Bob shook his said and added, "What now?"

Margarite hesitated, then, in a voice that betrayed her frustration, said. "We go there tonight."

Bob said, "I guess we have no other choice."

Margarite stiffened up and glared at him. Bob could see that her jaw was clenched, and she was working to control herself. Her demeanor bewildered him. They were both frustrated with events and were working towards the same conclusion. Why should she be looking at him with such anger? He decided silence was his best option.

After what seemed like a long time, she motioned for Bob to follow her. She led him into a corner of the barn away from the others. She grabbed him by the upper arm and, standing rigidly before him, she said in a harsh whisper, "Do you really not understand what all this means to me?"

Cautiously, Bob answered, "I thought I did."

"I had a handle on the cartels working in Chihuahua. I was able to track what they were doing and pass on useful and actionable intelligence. I knew something was changing, but that's nothing new. Something with these cartels is always changing. We were adjusting." Here she paused and took a few breaths before continuing. "Then here comes you, a gringo Lone Ranger hell bent on bringing American justice to poor Mexico. My operation is now going to be exposed. All the hard work of twenty years is ruined. It will take another twenty years to rebuild it."

Bob tried to interject. "I'm sorry I did not ..."

She held up her hand. "Stop, this is not about you. You don't understand. I was doing something that helped my country. Something that was meaningful on a large scale. Now I'm exposing my operation and my team in order to track down one girl. Do you understand, my entire operation is being put in jeopardy because of one girl? We have an expression in Mexico, I'll not bother you with the Spanish, but in English it is 'Poor Mexico so far from God and so close to the United States.' Don't you see, that's us. I'm Mexico, and you're the United States."

Bob felt duly chastised and genuinely worried he had done something terribly wrong. He realized he had shrunk to a somewhat submissive posture. As he thought about it, he straightened up, raised his eyes to look Margarite in the eye, and said, "I'm genuinely sorry for anything I have done to jeopardize your operation or your team."

She was still mad. "Do you understand how bad this is?"

Bob had had enough; he answered firmly but without hauteur. "Margarite, I didn't just fall off the turnip truck. I've spent most of my adult life serving a cause bigger than myself, just as you have. I used to think my mission was to fix everything, the Army, society, all of it. The trouble was when I tried to tilt at those windmills, all I did was break my lance. What I finally learned was that I had no influence on the greater world. Hell, the greater world didn't even know I existed. That dose of humility may be the most important lesson I have learned. I learned to focus on my world. That world was my family, my soldiers, my ranch, and a few special people who became part of my world. That hasn't changed. It's still my world. It's still my responsibility. All the energy and effort I put into saving the world is now focused on my world. Whether I like it or not, Luna has entered my world. I'm going after her, and I might—just might be able to save her." Here Bob paused, softened his voice, and said, "If you want to ride Rosinante off on your quest to save Mexico, that's your business, and I wish you luck."

Margarite was still mad, but she said. "Let's go, we need to work out the details of this evening's foolishness."

"OK," he answered."

CHAPTER NINETEEN

Near Janos, Chihuahua, Mexico, June 1996

Luna's plan to improve her condition was working. By choking back her revulsion whenever Don Poncho took her, and by forcing a smile on occasion, she had softened his attitude towards her. Her food was better, she had clean, or at least cleaner, bedding, and Poncho had not beaten her for a couple of days.

As she was considering her plight, Don Poncho entered the shed and said. "You should bathe and put on clean clothes. Can I trust you not to run if I unshackle you?"

This was so unexpected that she was unable to answer. He was starting to get perturbed by her lack of response. Luna saw this, and before Don Poncho lost his temper, she blurted out. "Yes, yes, you can trust me not to run."

Satisfied by her answer, he unlocked her shackles, handed her a bundle of clothes, a towel, soap, shampoo, and other odds and ends of toiletries. "Come with me," he said, and led her to the house.

The house was a large, old adobe with lots of large timber support beams and Iron furnishings. It was from an era of large ranches of hundreds of thousands of acres owned by rich hacendados. The hacienda had suffered from a lack of upkeep; in fact, over half the building was in ruins, just melted adobe walls, fallen timbers, rusted iron, and broken roof tiles. It didn't shine with its former resplendence, but half of the grand old hacienda was still functional. It held traces of its past glory, evident in what was left of the tile mosaic on the floor, and of the faded fresco murals on the plaster walls of the great room. Luna stopped to stare; she was taken aback. She had never seen anything so grand.

The mosaic on the floor was made up of small tiles carefully placed in an intricate geometric pattern. The walls were murals, or rather one large mural that extended around the room. It was a tableau of historic images, as if in a story. First was an Aztec Warrior in his elaborate headdress on a mountain peak, standing protectively over a beautiful young woman at his feet. On the ground with the young woman was the warrior's broken bow and a quiver of arrows. The warrior's arms were outstretched and raised with his palms up while his face, lifted to the sun, appeared to be pleading. Riding away from the Aztek warrior was a procession of conquistadores on horseback with priests carrying the cross before them and Indians being led behind.

Continuing to wrap around the room, the mural had scenes of Indians, peasant farmers, elegant caballeros on spirited horses, roping wild animals, and vaqueros working cattle. The last scene in the mural was of nineteenth-century soldiers defending the flag of Mexico. None of that was all that meaningful to Luna. Suddenly, she sucked in her breath; there was the image of Our Lady of Guadalupe on the wall over a small shrine. There was usually nothing unusual or bad about a shrine to Our Lady; there were shrines dedicated to the Virgin Mother throughout Mexico, but this shrine beneath the fresco of Our Lady had the bust of a man with a white shirt and black bandana. Luna looked at Don Poncho questioningly, and he said, "It's Jesus Malverde, El Santo Narco." Luna had been a conscientious young catholic, going to mass and completing her catechism; she had never heard of such a saint.

A large table was next to the Santo Narco shrine, and when she realized what it was, she gasped, "Brujas." On it were two human skulls, several bowls, beads, jars filled with nothing she recognized except maybe an eye. There was a knife and bundles of herbs. This was a place of evil, a place where Santeria shared power with the Virgin Mother. The mural was old, but the shrine and table were new. She felt her insides quiver as she stared at the shrine.

She was only vaguely aware of Don Poncho, who was now standing close to Malverde's shrine. He bowed, mumbled something to El Narco Santo, and crossed himself; then, returning to Luna, he nudged her shoulder, bringing her back to reality. "Hey, come with me." He showed her into the bathroom, pointing to the large claw-foot bathtub that was already filled with hot water, and said, "Bathe, make yourself pretty." He added with a knowing smile that made her dread what was coming. "You have important guests to meet tonight."

+++

That evening, the important guests arrived at Rancho de Nuestra Señora de Guadalupe. Don Poncho had her sit on a straight-backed chair across the room from where he sat with the three guests. Luna could see that one of these three was important to Don Poncho, who spoke to him deferentially, always using the formal forms of speech to address him, even calling him El Señor Andre. She didn't understand what the other two did. They just stood and kept looking all around. They didn't seem to be important.

The man called Andre spoke Spanish with a foreign accent. He seemed to be a friend of Don Poncho's. The other two men looked like gringos. One spoke Spanish with the same foreign accent as Andre. The three gringos spoke to each other in a language that was not Spanish, and as far as Luna could tell, did not sound like the English she had heard on TV or in the movies.

After an hour of talking, Don Poncho shook hands with El Señor Andre, then poured glasses of tequila, and raising his glass said, "Salud."

The guests raised their glasses in return and said, "Na Zdorovie."

+++

Bob, Margarite, and her operatives had crept up close to the old hacienda of Rancho de Nuestra Señora de Guadalupe. There was a beat-up pickup in the yard, but no other signs of life. They had already searched the outbuildings, and other than the disturbing evidence that the shed was used as a lockup for human trafficking, they had found nothing of interest. It was now time to enter the house.

Margarite sent her operators to cover the back and sides of the house as prearranged. She and Bob would enter the main house. She loaned Bob a pistol, saying, "Don't go all Clint Eastwood on me, shooting everyone in sight."

"No sweat. You point them out, then I'll shoot them."

"Bob, you're a true pain in the ass."

"Oh, PITA, is it. I do my best."

Due to the suspected presence of Luna or other captives, they elected to do a stealthy rather than a violent entry to the main house. Margarite was preparing to pick the lock when she gently pushed on the large double door; it yielded. This was disconcerting. She and Bob quietly slipped into the hacienda. They were in a large room lit only by a sputtering candle on a table. They quietly scanned the great room in search of threats. Once Margarite was sure the room was clear, she waved Bob over. She pointed at the shrine and whispered, "It's a shrine to

Malverde." She then touched some of the small votive candle holders on the shrine. "They're still warm."

Margarite motioned for Bob to follow her to a door at the far end of the room. The door encroached on the room's large mural. It created a gap between a procession of priests and conquistadores on one side and a column of Mexican lancers on the other side. The lancers rode under a banner with the date 1821 on it. Margarite and Bob positioned themselves on either side of the door, and Margarite tried the doorknob. It turned, so she pushed it open and passed through with Bob close on her heels. They found themselves in a hallway with doors on one side and windows on the other. All the doors were wide open except the last one. It was slightly ajar.

Easing down the hallway, they quietly cleared each room as they passed. When they reached the last room, Bob peered through the slight opening in the door. He pulled back and pointed to his eyes, held up one finger, and drew the finger across his throat. Margarite pushed the door open, and they entered with guns raised. There was only one occupant in the room. He was dead.

Satisfied that there was no danger, nor any captives present, Margarite ordered a thorough sweep of the grounds and hacienda in search of clues. When finished, they had nothing except tire tracks and a cluster of footprints in the drive where a vehicle had been parked. The tracks were those of at least two men and probably more. There was also one female. Bob saw that something was telling about the men's footprints. None of the prints were of cowboy boots. He pointed all this out to Margarite. "Bob," she said. "You're a cowboy, you must be a decent tracker.

"I get by."

She asked Bob to look at the tracks more closely. He saw nothing different than the others had until he spotted one pair of distinctive prints where someone had stepped to the edge of the drive to pee. He said, "These are city boys. The prints reminded me of shoes I saw in Europe." More importantly, when he checked the wet dirt, it hadn't cooled to the air temperature yet. Bob stood with a sense of urgency, saying, "They were just here; the piss is still warmer than the dirt we missed them by minutes."

Margarite shouted, "Let's go." The team piled into the Ramcharger SUV and raced down the long drive until they reached an intersection of the main highway. Stopping to check for any indication of which way the traffickers had gone, Bob saw the obvious sign of fresh dusty tire tracks turning onto the paved highway from the dirt drive. They were headed east.

As they raced down the highway to catch up with Luna, Bob said, "So far, Rancho de Nuestra Señora de Guadalupe held only a corpse, a shrine to a bogus patron saint of Narcos, an altar to evil magic, and evidence of human trafficking. He added sarcastically, "The Lady of Guadalupe must be pissed the fuck off. Her name has been used to mask the worst kind of evil—she sure lost her virginity in this place."

Margarite shot a disapproving look at Bob. It was wrong to speak in such a crass manner about the virgin mother. She started to revile him for his disrespect, but then took in a breath and said, "Sadley, in spite of your offensive phrasing, I think you're right."

CHAPTER TWENTY

New Mexico, United States, Chihuahua, Mexico, border, June 1996

After leaving Rancho de Nuestra Señora de Guadalupe and the body of Don Poncho behind, Andre and his men had driven fast. Soon, the path they took left paved roads behind, avoiding towns, ranches, or anything that looked occupied.

It had only been a few hours ago that the three men had killed Don Poncho and taken Luna when the SUV pulled over next to a white van. It was a passenger van with rows of seats and windows. One of the men, Yuri, who appeared to be the number two man, took Luna by the arm and shoved her into the van. He climbed into the front passenger seat. From here, the van led the way, and the SUV followed. Luna was in the back of the van with other young women, being driven down a dusty back road.

Before dawn, the van stopped at a five-wire fence that ran east to west. It was straight and long with a six-foot-tall white obelisk on the south side of it, and a road running parallel to it on the north side. The driver opened the chain link gate and drove through, closing the gate behind.

As they drove by the obelisk, one of the young women whispered, "Estados Unidos." The women who had been in the van when Luna joined them seemed happy. Luna was confused;

she was not happy. She didn't want to be in el otro lado. She wanted to be home.

It was here that the SUV accompanying them pulled ahead and led the way. A few miles further, they pulled into a driveway where they were greeted by a man and woman who guided them to a barn behind the house where they parked the vehicles. Once inside, the women were taken out of the vehicles and led to the house where they were fed breakfast and given the opportunity to wash up and use the bathroom. It was here that the vehicles were washed to remove the road dirt and had their Chihuahua license plates changed out. The SUV put on a US government plates, and the van put on a commercial New Mexico plate. The van also had a magnetic sign put on either side, 'Texas, New Mexico Transit'. In smaller letters on the second line, it said, 'Deming, Las Cruces, Hatch, El Paso'. The sign also had an 800 phone number. One of the men stenciled a US Department of Transportation number on the bumper.

The man who greeted them at the ranch was in serious conversation with Andre. They were speaking a language that Luna did not recognize as English; it was the same language Andre used to speak to his two men. Luna started to get worried, but she was hungry, the breakfast was good, and the other women were happy and began to chat with each other. It seemed harmless enough. What Luna did know was that this was better than anything she'd dealt with over the past several weeks.

The woman cooking breakfast listened to the women from the van and began to ask a few questions, such as where the women were from, whether they were excited about coming to the north, and other chit-chat. Luna thought the woman looked like she might be Mexican, like the women on the Mexican Telenovelas were Mexican with their fair skin and light brown or blond hair. To Luna, her Spanish was strange. It was more than just a strange accent. She used some English words, mixed with some words that weren't Spanish and didn't sound English. She spoke with some archaic forms that resembled the language of the old Reina-Valera Bible her priest would read from. When asked, she said her name was Marcial, and she was from a small town near Taos, New Mexico. Her questions were innocuous enough, but Luna had learned to keep quiet.

The other women from the van were traveling north by choice. The driver of the van was a coyote they had paid to bring them to America, where they were promised high-paying modeling jobs. He told them he had contacts that would provide them with green cards so they would be able to work without the danger of deportation. They were on their way to the land of their dreams. They would be rich and be able to send lots of money to their families. It was wonderful. Their trip would be over soon. Luna was not so sure.

+++

Bob and Margarite were standing in the middle of the dirt road where the tracks of the vehicle they suspected of carrying Luna were mixed with the tracks of another vehicle and some footprints. From this point, the new vehicle led the way towards the border.

Margarite looked up from the tracks and said, "They're headed to the Border."

"And this is nowhere near Juarez, is it?"

"No, and it doesn't look like they have any intention of going there. My men say this is an unmapped road used by smugglers. It goes to the border where there is a gate. We're not far from there now, maybe an hour. If they keep going in this direction, they'll cross about twenty-five miles west of Columbus." Margarite turned to face Bob in the headlights of their vehicle. "I can't go north of the border with you; neither can my men."

"I understand about your men, but you're a US citizen. You can cross the border."

"I'm not authorized to operate in the US, you know that. Besides, I have a lot of work to do here...even more now. I'll make a call and arrange a pickup for you." With that, she returned to the vehicle to place the sat phone call.

Bob stopped her and asked. "Can your contact intercept them when they cross?"

"No, but I'll try and get a tail on them if we can identify the vehicles."

"Thanks."

After getting off the phone, Margarite told Bob. "There's a shipping corral on the north side of the Border near the gate that this road goes to. Your contact will meet you there. It's only a few miles below NM Highway 9. They can go in three directions once they are on Highway 9. They can go east to El Paso, west to Hachita, or north to Deming."

Bob asked, "What do you think is most likely?"

"North to Deming. West makes no sense; it's a long way to a metropolitan area. East is dangerous for them; the highway along the border to El Paso is heavily patrolled by La Migra. North on the old railroad grade to Deming is my guess. It gives them lots of options. I'll tell you about them in the car. Let's go."

+++

After everyone had eaten breakfast, the girls loaded into the van with the coyote driving and Yuri in the passenger seat. The SUV was driven by Fyador with Andre in the front passenger seat. As they pulled away from the ranch house, the two vehicles fell in behind a water truck being driven by the man from the

183

ranch. He was sprinkling water on the dirt driveway and the quarter mile of unpaved road leading to the highway. There would be no telltale dust on the vehicles.

As the Van and SUV were about to turn onto NM Highway 9, a beat-up pickup truck turned off the highway and passed them heading in the opposite direction. There was nothing suspicious about the old truck. It was typical of many of the ranch trucks in the area, well-worn by miles of use on tough roads.

The driver of the pickup noted the other three vehicles with interest. A truck watering the road was not too uncommon, but being followed by a passenger van and an SUV with government plates was odd.

When the pickup driver had traveled just a few hundred yards down the dirt road, he noted the driveway on the left side of the road. Both the drive and the dirt road were damp from watering, but not the road to the south. The driver stopped and took a quick look. The tracks of two vehicles followed the water truck out of the drive and north on the dirt road towards the highway. This may be important. The driver noted the location and continued to his rendezvous with the Margarite on the border.

The meeting between Margarite and John, the pickup driver, was brief. There was a quick exchange of information after which Bob thanked Margarite and her men and started to get in the pickup to head north and find Luna. Margarite stopped him. "Bob, good luck. I hope you find this girl and whatever else you're looking for." One of her men then handed her two packages. One was long and rolled in a blanket. The other was a gym bag. "We retrieved these from your Amish friend. You're on your own side of the border now. You can have your weapons back."

Bob asked, "What about the horse and tack?"

"I've arranged for it to be returned."

Bob smiled, gave her an unexpected hug, and said, "Thank you."

When John started the truck, Bob could feel the power of the engine. This was no old beater. In addition to a powerful engine, there was a sophisticated communication setup with a police radio scanner, a CB radio, an HF radio, and a satellite phone.

As they started north, John said, "About a mile north of here is a ranch. When I was on the way down, an SUV and a van came out of there and headed north to Highway 9. The van was white and had New Mexico commercial plates. There was a sign on the side. I didn't get a good look at it, but it was some sort of shuttle service. The SUV was black and had government plates. When I saw them, they were following a water truck. Their tracks followed the water truck from the ranch drive."

Bob said, "Then we're close. Can we catch them?"

"Do you know where they're going?"

"Margarite thinks, Demming."

"I'll try. We'll check to see if they have turned east or west. It's cool enough that there should still be wet tracks where they turned off onto the highway. I'll call the border patrol and see if they can keep an eye out for them."

While John was talking to the border patrol on the radio, they arrived at the intersection of the dirt road and NM9. John stopped, and Bob got out to examine the road. He found what he was looking for. While the water truck went west, dripping some water, in what may have been an effort to deceive pursuers, the wet tracks of two other vehicles went east.

Bob hurried back to the pickup and said, "They've gone east."

John said, "The Border Patrol will set up a checkpoint west of Columbus, but that leaves the Hermanas Grade, an old railroad grade that goes to Deming. They don't have anybody that far from Columbus this morning. We'll go that way and see if we can catch up to them. I have a contact in the Sheriff's department. I'll see if they can watch for them on the Hermanas Grade." With that, John accelerated.

+++

As the SUV and van turned off NM9 onto the old railroad grade road passing a small feed lot, the vehicles' drivers sped up. The SUV pulled away from the van. It would act as the scout. The road was straight, lightly traveled, and, based on information they had, not patrolled much by the local police. This was an opportunity to cover ground fast. Soon they would be back on busy highways and passing through towns and cities where they had to be careful not to draw attention. Here they appeared to be alone.

The country was Chihuahua desert scrub, made up of creosote, acacia, and other desert shrubs mixed with some grasses, an assortment of bush muley under the shrubs with a mix of curly mesquite and various grammas on the better soil, with tobosa in the heavy, soiled flats and sacaton in the wash bottoms.

Like much of the southwest, there were rugged mountains scattered around. The morning sky was a brilliant blue that would change to an almost white sky with the afternoon's intense heat, and almost overpoweringly, brilliant sun. There were small white puffs, almost no more than hints of clouds, over some of the mountains. The monsoon storms would not build from them until later in the afternoon.

Luna was tired. In the last twenty-four hours, Don Poncho had unlocked her from being cuffed to a pipe in a filthy shed, let her bathe, put on clean clothes, and introduced her to three men who then killed Don Poncho and kidnapped her. The irony of being kidnapped from her kidnapper was not lost on Luna. All this and the fact that her life had been in total turmoil for several weeks had left her exhausted. Her mind went back and forth between giving in completely to whatever these men wanted or jumping out of the van at her first chance.

Suddenly, there was a call on the CB radio. Yuri answered and spoke in the language that Luna had heard earlier, but did not recognize. Whatever was said upset him. In broken Spanish, he told the driver to pull over at once and remove the signs from the side of the van.

After the van was stopped on the side of the road, Yuri explained to the driver." There is a checkpoint ahead. Andre will be back here soon. They will turn on the SUV's emergency police lights and siren. We will follow them through the checkpoint." The driver spoke to the women, telling them to stay calm, sit straight, and not look at anyone on the road.

CHAPTER TWENTY-ONE

Luna County, New Mexico, United States, June 1996

The pickup had travelled north on Hermanas Grade for a dozen miles when they noticed flashing lights a mile ahead. The lights appeared to be from a single vehicle. Other vehicles, further north, were rushing south at high speed with sirens and flashing lights. Something was wrong. John immediately tuned the pickup's scanner to the Luna County Sheriff's dispatcher frequency. The chatter was about shots fired involving one of their deputies on Hermanas Grade.

John began slowing down and flashing his headlights. When the pickup stopped, it was about a half mile from the single vehicle with flashing lights. They could see it was a police cruiser. It was in the middle of the road, lying broadside to traffic. By this time, the vehicles coming from the north had arrived at the scene. John got out of the pickup, stood by the driver's door with the radio mike in his hand, and transmitted. "This is the pickup on the Hermanas Grade just south of you." As he said this, he waved his arm. "We are two. We want to approach. We have useful information."

One of the vehicles pulled away from the cluster of flashing lights and headed towards them. John told Bob to get out and stand in front of the truck. It was a short wait for the Sheriff's car. Bob had pulled his Cochise County Deputy Sheriff's badge from his pocket and held it in plain sight. John looked at him with surprise and said, "I didn't know you were a cop."

Bob smiled. "I'm not, not really, until now."

"Margarite said you'd get me into the shit. She also said I could trust you, so OK, Deputy."

+++

After running the checkpoint and exchanging gunfire with the lone Luna County deputy, the SUV had turned off Hermanas Grade onto a dirt road with the van close behind. Both vehicles were speeding away from the scene at breakneck speed. With wounds from flying glass to his face and left arm, the driver of the van was struggling to maintain control. His companion Yuri was crumpled forward in the passenger footwell, wedged between the door and the engine cover. Much of his brain and skull were splattered across the front windshield. One of the young women in the back was bleeding heavily from a wound in her thigh. Several others had cuts from shattered glass. The van was struggling to keep up when one of the front tires blew out.

Luna and the other young women in the van were desperately gripping the seats, clinging to each other—just grasping for anything to keep from flying around the inside of the van as it careened nearly out of control down the road. Dust and wind poured through the shattered windows, making a whirlwind of choking air. This, with the overwhelming sounds of rushing wind and battered machinery crashing along the road, accompanied by the screams of panicked women, the cries of the wounded, and Andrei's insistent demands coming over the CB radio to keep up, was chaos. Luna thought this must be hell; it can't be worse. She was wrong.

She was suddenly aware that the violent bouncing and swaying of the van had stopped. She had the feeling of floating. Then there was the smashing impact of hitting something unmovable at high speed, followed by flipping over and over while crashing around inside the van, then nothing, just darkness.

Andrei saw the van lose control and run off the road, running over the roadside berm, which launched into the air. It traveled in an arc for over seventy feet, smashed down at a steep angle, then flipped end over end for another fifty feet. He shouted. "Fyador, turn around. Go back to the van. Hurry!"

Andrei knew he should have simply continued without turning back, but he had so much at stake with these women. The Jarez cartel had fronted him the money with his promises of large profits and his personal warrant against loss. He had played on the reputation of the Russian mob's experience and success in the human trafficking business. Now he had not only lost his investment, but he was also going to be on the cartel's hit list. He didn't have much time to think about any of this as Fyador slid to a stop at the site of the wreck.

+++

Bob was looking out the window as the pickup pulled away from the site of the shooting. A deputy had been shot, but his wound was not too serious. He had returned fire. He was sure he had hit the van. Automotive glass on the road confirmed this.

"John, none of the cops that responded to the shooting saw an SUV or van north of here. They must have turned off. Where could they do that?"

"Just up ahead, there's lots of irrigated agriculture with an extensive grid of roads."

Bob said. "They must have gone that way. Let's try that."

John took a right off the Hermanas Grade at a large circle pivot irrigated farm field. "Bob, all these roads are dirt or gravel. They will be making dust, especially if they are traveling fast. My guess is they'll turn north soon. It's only another half dozen miles of flats before the roads end at the mountains. Keep an eye out for dust clouds."

+++

Andrei and Fyador rushed from the SUV towards the wreckage of the van. Yuri was dead, and the driver was in a bad way but alive. Yuri killed him. Andrei said, "We need to find any of the women who aren't hurt too bad and take them with us."

As the two men looked over the scene of wreckage, all they found were three dead women, and one with her legs shattered and bent back at sickening angles. She was conscious, and shock had set in. Andrei looked at Fyador. "She's no good to us, you know what to do—no loose ends."

They continued their search and came upon Luna. She was unconscious but breathing. She had been thrown from the van, but there were no apparent signs of massive injury. She had survived. Fyador revived her with slaps and shouting. Once she came to Andrei and Fyador lifted her to her feet and started towards the SUV.

A rising dust cloud to the south caught Andrei's attention. It was a mile or two away. Somebody was coming up the road towards them. Judging from the height of the dust cloud and its rate of advance, whoever they were, they were moving fast. Andrei was still missing two women; he couldn't take the time to look for them. He'd have to hope they were dead. "Hurry, we have company, we have to get out of here." They ran to the SUV, dragging Luna along.

+++

Bob and John had only traveled about a mile when they saw the hint of dust in the air to their north. It wasn't much, but it was all they had. John turned north at the next road. As they traveled north, the dust in the air became a little thicker. There was no wind, so dust would linger and not drift away from the roadway. Something had gone up this road recently.

After a few more miles, they came to a slight rise in the road that gave them an unobstructed view to the north. "There!" Said Bob. "See it?" Ahead was a dust cloud rising over the road, trailing behind a black SUV speeding north.

John increased his speed to try and catch the SUV. As the pickup gained speed, John and Bob settled in for the final part of the chase. Bob checked his pistol and reached behind the seat for his Mauser.

Suddenly, John hit the brakes. They slid to a stop in a cloud of dust. Looking out the side of the truck, they could see the van over a hundred feet from the road, lying on its side with windows smashed, and the roof caved in. There was detritus scattered from the road to the van. What appeared to be bodies, clothes, and paper marked the area from where the van had hit the ground to its final resting place. Bob hadn't seen anything like this since Vietnam. He was struck by its similarity to the aftermath of a bloody battle. Trash and paper were scattered over the site among the bodies. The movies never got that right.

Bob and John rushed from the pickup to the crash scene. They hoped to find survivors but found corpses. They found four dead women, one of whom had a fresh bullet wound to the head. Both the driver of the van and another man were dead from apparent bullet wounds. There was a young woman partially under the van; she was unconscious but not dead.

John said, "Call for help on the truck's radio. It's tuned to the Luna County Sheriff's office. I'll stay here and do what I can for her. Please hurry."

After calling for help, Bob grabbed some water and a medical bag from behind the seat and a shovel from the truck bed. He hurried back to the van, quickly checking each of the dead women as he passed them. None could be Luna. He'd never seen her, but he knew she was only fourteen or fifteen at most. These women were in their twenties.

When he got to the van, John was talking to the young woman pinned under the van. She was fortunate in that the van had landed in soft soil, pinning her underneath. She was injured, but in pretty good spirits, trusting that she would now be all right.

John said, "Now give me a hand. I need to start an IV and dig out some of this dirt under her head so she can be a little more comfortable." After getting the IV started, John said, "Here, support her head while I clear some of this dirt away."

Bob did as asked. While John carefully dug. Bob said, "Why don't we just dig her out? We can do that."

John looked uncomfortable. "She may be suffering crush injuries. She's already been under this van for at least ten minutes. How long until help arrives?"

"They said cops soon, ambulance twenty to thirty minutes."

"We have to wait for the medics to arrive. Removing the pressure could kill her."

"Shit, what can I do?"

John said, "After we get her head in a better position, see if you can find any others."

"OK, but please ask her if there was a girl named Luna."

John did not like the idea of questioning this young woman. He believed she was going to die, and he only wanted to keep her comfortable. He said he'd do what he could.

As Bob left to search for the missing girl, he could hear John speaking Spanish to the injured woman. He sounded upbeat, and Bob was sure he understood. John ask her if he could take her dancing after she got better. She had answered something about being honored to dance with such a handsome gentleman. Her words were caballero guapo.

Bob found a body several yards from the truck. The young woman had been thrown clear. It was plain she had a broken neck; he could do nothing for her. She was too old to be Luna. He started working his way back towards the road, looking for anything significant. He saw two sets of footprints. They were men's. He followed them for several yards and came across a place where there were signs of activity. The footprints were scrambled; it looked as if someone had been lying on the ground. At this point, the men's tracks were joined by a small set of footprints.

Bob followed the tracks to the road, where they met up with a set of tire tracks on the shoulder and disappeared onto the road. He gathered up some more water and carried it back to John. As he approached the wrecked van, he heard sirens in the distance. Things were about to get complicated.

John was talking reassuringly to the young woman under the van. She was not in much pain, but she was becoming distressed and weaker. Bob sat next to John and said, "I found one dead woman over there, with a broken neck. Back towards the road, there are two sets of men's tracks and one small set of tracks leading back to the road. They ended at a set of tire tracks."

John said. "So, you think that's the missing girl?"

"Yeah."

Handing Bob the keys, John said. "OK, get out of here. Take the truck. Use the satellite phone in the truck to call Jane. Bring her up to speed. Good Luck."

"Thank you." Bob looked at the young woman. He knew she was dying. John knew she was dying, but John was not going to let her die alone. Bob put his hand on John's shoulder and started to speak, but nothing came out. Finally, he said, "You know."

"Yeah, I know."

CHAPTER TWENTY-TWO

Southwest New Mexico, United States, June 1996

The SUV was passing through Deming, New Mexico. Andrei had been poring over a map, trying to find a way to Albuquerque using back roads to avoid the interstates. The shootout with the police meant law enforcement would be on alert. He had to assume that whoever was in the pickup that stopped at the scene of the van wreck had seen the SUV depart. By now, the description of the SUV and its direction of travel would have been sent to all the law enforcement agencies in the Southwest. His only chance of getting away was to get another vehicle.

Stealing or carjacking a vehicle at nine o'clock in the morning was risky. They couldn't do it in Deming. It would have to be done away from town. Andrei had an idea. "Fyador, turn right here, then we turn left onto Highway 180. It's not far. Go north on 180 for a little over a mile, then turn right onto Highway 26.

Luna was staring out the back window as they drove through Deming. She hurt all over. She had taken a beating in the van when it smashed into the ground, and flipped over, tossing her and the others around like beans inside a rattle, smashing into seats, the van's interior, and each other. After being ejected, she had lain unconscious in the dirt until Andrei and Fyador came. Now she was in the SUV again, and they were passing through a town. She was staring out the window. There are people here.

I should get out and call for help, she thought. When she tried the door handle, it was locked. The child lock had been set. Andrei reached back, grabbed her arm, and told her she was going nowhere.

In less than an hour, the SUV was pulled over on the shoulder of Highway 26. Fyador had raised the hood and was bent over as if checking the engine. Andrei was standing in the road waving his arms, trying to flag down an approaching pickup. He had already dismissed a couple of offers for help. He wasn't interested in a small sedan or a minivan. The pickup he was focused on was a white, late-model, four-wheel drive with an extended cab. Perhaps the most common vehicle in the Southwest.

The driver pulled over in front of the SUV and got out, offering to help. When he got close to the SUV, Andrei pulled his pistol. Fyador grabbed him and shoved him to the ground, using the SUV to shield him from the road while holding his pistol on him. When asked, he said the keys were in the truck. Andrei checked and confirmed they were. With that, Fyador shoved him into the front seat of the SUV and shot him. Pulling Luna from the back seat, Fyador dragged her to the pickup and shoved her into the back seat as Andrei punched the accelerator, spinning his tires on the gravel shoulder. Fyador had to run a few long steps while holding onto the pickup's passenger door and jumped into the truck.

Once they had a little distance between them and the dead man in the SUV, Andrei slowed down to the speed limit. While getting away fast was important, it was not worth the risk of being pulled over by the police.

+++

No one knew where the SUV had gone, so all the possible roads out of Deming needed to be covered. That was a lot of roads, a lot of miles, and not a lot of assets. Agencies as diverse as four county sheriff's departments, a few municipal police departments, the New Mexico State Police, and the Border Patrol were involved. There were even calls out requesting the US Forest Service law enforcement officers and New Mexico Game wardens keep their eyes open.

Trooper Santiago was racing southwest on Highway 26, known as the Hatch Cutoff. He needed to set up a roadblock at Nutt that would cover both the Hatch Cutoff and the 27 road that ran north. There was a white pickup a couple of miles away coming his way. The truck was not suspicious, traveling at a reasonable speed and not matching the description of the suspect vehicle. Trooper Santiago slowed down so he could get a better look as they closed the distance. Suddenly, there was a call on the radio. The Black SUV had been found. There was a dead civilian in the vehicle. A carjacking was suspected.

Trooper Santiago turned on his emergency lights, preparing to stop and, if necessary, engage the occupants of the truck. The truck accelerated. It was trying to get to Nutt and turn off onto 27 before he could block them. He pushed the gas to the floor to close the distance and try to get to the turn ahead of them. During all this, he was on the radio reporting the situation.

Trooper Santiago was not going to be able to block the intersection ahead of the white pickup. He knew it was a risk, but the stakes were high. While traveling at far too high a speed for such a maneuver, he cut across the bare dirt patch that passed as a parking lot for Nutt. He passed the Nutt Bar, trailing a cloud of dust, when his rear end broke loose, causing him to lose control. Regaining control after fishtailing, he managed to dodge the RVs parked under the metal roof and thread the needle between two trees before he took out a fence post and four strands of barbed wire, sliding to a stop on the far side of the 27 road, facing straight at the approaching white pickup truck.

The white pickup had already committed to the turn onto the 27 road. When the trooper's car crashed through the fence and skidded to a stop, Fyador was doing his best not to lose control while making a high-speed turn. He punched the accelerator when the truck straightened out, passing over the cattle guard. The combination of the steel rails of the cattle guard, the force of the turn, and the power of the truck's big engine broke traction. The white pickup did a complete 360-degree spin, ending up on the shoulder of the 27 road.

Trooper Santiago and Adrei were staring at each other. Both immediately had their weapons out. Santiago hesitated, seeing Luna in the truck seated behind Andrei. He didn't have a clear shot. As he dove for cover behind his dash, his windshield exploded. As the glass showered down on him, Trooper Santiago heard the rev of the pickup's engine and the sound of tires spinning on dirt as the truck tried to accelerate. He sat up as the truck regained the pavement. Trooper Santiago had one shot. He took it.

CHAPTER TWENTY-THREE

Southwest New Mexico, United States, June 1996

Bob had pulled into a gas station in Deming. There were lots of options on where to go from here, and he had no idea which one the SUV had taken. He was leaning towards taking the Hatch Cutoff to I-25 as most likely. Whatever way they had gone, he didn't want to start without topping off his gas tank. He had been monitoring the police scanner. There was lots of chatter about the shooting on the Hermanas Grade and the wrecked van. The call was out to watch for the black SUV with two armed males and one female hostage, but nothing on recent sightings or possible routes.

Bob had placed a call to Jane. He gave her the executive summary of what had happened. He promised more details when he had time. Now he needed information on where the SUV was going. She passed on to him the information from John. The injured girl under the wrecked van had told John the men in the SUV were not Mexicans or Americans. She thought they were European. With that and previous information, Jane suspected they were Russians. While she was talking to him, a call came over the radio. A Luna County Sheriff's deputy had found an SUV on the Hatch Cutoff. Someone had jacked a vehicle and killed the driver. As he pulled out of the gas station,

Bob told Jane what he had just heard on the scanner and said he'd keep her posted.

Bob left Deming and turned onto Highway 26 towards the town of Hatch. The Hatch Cutoff is a wide two-lane highway with long straight stretches and few curves. Taking advantage of this, Bob had the truck running at over ninety miles per hour. Ahead, he saw flashing emergency lights. He slowed as he approached the sheriff's cruiser and a black SUV. There was a sheriff's deputy talking on the radio while looking through the driver's side door. Bob slowed nearly to a stop. He needed to know if Luna was in the vehicle. He offered to help the deputy, hoping to get a little time to look over the scene. He saw a man's body on the front seat, nothing more. The deputy said help was on the way and hustled Bob on with a wave.

A few miles beyond where Bob saw the black SUV on the side of the road, another call came over the scanner. A New Mexico State Trooper was declaring an officer-involved shooting at Nutt, the intersection of the Hatch Cutoff and the 27 road. The suspect vehicle was a late-model white Ram Pickup with two men and a woman. They were now going northwest on the 27 road towards Lake Valley. Bob passed a sign "Nutt 10 miles, Hatch 28 miles".

Bob slowed down just enough to make the turn on the 27 road when he saw Trooper Santiago waving him to a stop just past the cattle guard. He jammed on the brakes and stopped with the tires screeching on the asphalt. As the smoke cleared, the Trooper approached. Bob had to decide how to handle this. Should he bullshit his way through or just ignore the trooper and drive on? He decided to play it by ear.

Trooper Santiago was approaching Bob when he got a call on his cell phone. It was a short call, and when he was finished, he came up to the truck muttering to himself under his breath, "What the hell is going on? Must be some fed bull shit." Addressing Bob, he said. "I don't know who you are or who you know, but you're free to go."

"OK."

"I assume you're in pursuit of two men and a woman."

"Yep."

"They went through here less than ten minutes ago in a white Ram pickup. We exchanged shots. I may have hit the driver. The Sierra County Sheriff is sending someone to Hillsboro to block the intersection."

"Are you OK? Do you need help?"

The look on Trooper Santiago's face said it all. He was not pleased. "NO! I don't need any help."

"Thank you for the info." Bob sped off.

+++

Racing down the 27 road towards Lake Valley, Bob was trying to make sense out of the chatter on the police scanner with no luck. Weak and broken transmissions, combined with lots of traffic stepping on one another, along with the use of unfamiliar 10 codes, made the whole thing mostly incomprehensible to Bob. All he understood was that Grant County was sending someone west to an intersection at San Lorenzo to block access west and south.

Bob had only a passing familiarity with this part of New Mexico. He'd been on the 152 road many years earlier. He'd driven it from Silver City over the Black Range through Hillsboro to I-25 south of Truth or Consequences. From what he had gathered from the garbled radio traffic and the mileage sign, the 27 road must intersect with the 152 road at Hillsboro. Now he had a picture of what the police were trying to do. They wanted to isolate the Ram pickup truck by blocking potential exit routes.

+++

Luna saw that Fyador had been hit by a bullet fired by the policeman. From her seat in the back of the truck, she saw the blood soaking through the left shoulder of his suit coat. It was lots of blood spreading across his back. He spoke to Andrei in the language they often used. His voice sounded like he was getting tired.

Andrei had Fyador pull over. I'll drive from here. As Fyadori came unsteadily around the truck to get into the passenger seat, Andrei shot him, leaving him on the side of the road. After killing Fyador, Andrei moved Luna into the front passenger seat. He told her if she tried anything, he'd shoot her.

Staring at the desert grassland as it sped by, Luna's mind was working hard to sort everything out. After all the evil and misery she'd experienced from the time she'd been taken from her village to being locked in Don Poncho's shed, she thought she'd seen the worst there could be, but she found the chaos, death, and desperation of the past day to be unfathomable. It didn't seem real; it was like a bad dream, but it was real. She knew that her life was worth nothing to this man. She couldn't even understand why she was still alive. So many had died; why had she lived? She lived under no illusions about her future. She had none. The next crisis this man faced, he'd kill her in a heartbeat if it helped him to escape. She would have to take whatever opportunity she could to get away.

+++

The road was mostly straight with easy curves. It was fenced, so there shouldn't be any livestock ambling down the middle of the road. He monitored the gas level; he had well over half a tank. He thought that's plenty. Bob was pushing the pickup to a hundred miles per hour. The day was heating up, giving him cause for concern. The engine may have been tricked out, but he was asking a lot from it. He closely monitored engine temperature and oil pressure.

As he slowed for an approaching curve in the road that had a sign declaring "Lake Valley," he passed something out of place on the side of the road. It was a person lying on the shoulder of the road. He stopped the truck and backed up, hoping this was not the young woman he'd been trying to find. It wasn't; it was a man with a gunshot wound to his left shoulder. Bob checked the body for identification and saw that the bullet had passed through the man's shoulder, missing the bone, and lodging under the skin of his armpit against a rib. The second shot to the head was the fatal wound.

Bob stood and looked at the dead man. "So, you became a burden, and your boss killed you. Well, looks like it sucks to be you." Walking back to the pickup, Bob said to himself, "That means I have one victim and one asshole to track down."

As Bob approached Hillsboro, he saw the flashing lights of a police car pulling to a stop at the intersection. The sheriff's deputy stepped out of his car and flagged him to stop. Bob stopped and waited with his hands visible on the steering wheel. The deputy approached the pickup with caution and asked. "Have you seen a white pickup?"

"No."

"Where did you just come from?"

Bob thought this was an opportunity. Maybe he could get the deputy to think the white pickup was still back on the 27 road somewhere. "I came up from Lake Valley. Is something wrong?"

"No, just a traffic stop. License and registration, please."

This was not good. Bob's license was in good order, but he had no idea what the registration would say. He handed the deputy his license and was rummaging around in the glove box looking for the registration. As he pulled it out, the deputy got an urgent call on the radio. When he finished with the radio call, he handed Bob back his driver's license and said, "You're fine." Then he ran back to his car and started towards Lake Valley.

With a big sigh of relief, Bob put the unchecked registration back in the glove compartment. Well, the cop came up from the east, so Luna and her captor had to have gone west. Bob turned west on New Mexico 152 and gunned the engine. He felt he had a chance to catch up with them. This road went straight up into the Black Range. Other than a few forest service roads, four-wheel drive trails, and campground pull-offs offs there were no turn-offs before San Lorenzo. Bob remembered NM 152 as a typical mountain road with lots of sharp curves and its fair share of hairpin turns. It was his kind of road. Bob was confident he could catch Luna and the Russian.

+++

Luna needed to pee. She asked Andrei to stop and let her relieve herself. He had no intention of stopping. "You need to pee; you pee where you sit. I'm not stopping." Luna continued to protest and said she needed to do more than just pee; she had diarrhea. Peeing in the truck was one thing, but Andrei was not prepared to deal with that. He relented and pulled over by a cattle guard where the shoulder widened.

Luna went behind a Manzanita bush. Andrei told her to stay where he could see her. She argued and insisted on some privacy. She dropped as if to squat. Crouching, she started to move away quietly. Her plan was to go uphill. He was a strong man, but a man of the city. She, however, was raised in the mountains. She could outrun him.

Andrei became suspicious after just a minute or so, calling out to her and getting no answer. He rushed to check behind the manzanita. She was gone. It didn't take him long to see which way she had gone. He had to catch her. He knew he had a better chance of getting away if he left her behind, but he was obsessed with the idea of finishing with at least one of his charges. So much had gone wrong with his plan; he had to salvage something. Losing her would mean total failure. He would be seen as a man with no honor. That was unacceptable.

She heard him call for her. She started to run up the side of the hill. She had not gone far when she heard him shout to stop or he'd shoot. Looking over her shoulder, she considered whether to stop or not. He was aiming the pistol at her. She thought he might be too far for the shot. Should she stop or run?

Andrei knew she was at the extreme limit of his effective range with the pistol. He had an idea. He fired the pistol. The bullet kicked up dirt several feet to her right. He hollered at her. "That's a warning. The next will be to your heart." She didn't run anymore.

As Andrei pulled Luna back to the white pickup, he repeatedly slapped her, shouting, "Don't run away ever. I'll catch you and make you pay in pain. Understand?"

She whimpered. "Yes." He loaded her back into the pickup and pulled out onto the road.

CHAPTER TWENTY-FOUR

Black Range, Gila National Forest, New Mexico, United States, June 1996

A quarter of a mile to his left, across a canyon, Bob could see the road. It was higher up the mountain and parallel to him, going in the opposite direction, the result of a switchback. He saw a white pickup pull onto it from the shoulder. It was a late-model Ram pickup truck with two people. Bob knew the rough topography and frequent switchbacks would provide terrain masking he could use to close the distance without causing suspicion. He pressed a little harder on the accelerator. He had them.

Luna was disappointed in her failure to escape, but she knew she would have another chance. She was tired; she'd had no sleep for more than a day, or was it two? It seemed like a lifetime ago. She was tired of being abused. She was tired of being under the complete control of these monsters. Life like this was not worth living. She would try to escape again. If she died trying—well, that was an escape from the misery.

Andrei was getting frustrated with the road. He was muttering under his breath about not being a mountain goat. This road was a ridiculous collection of hairpin curves and long switchbacks. He had to drive two miles to gain one. Every time he had a straight stretch and managed to gain some speed, he'd have to hit the brakes for a sharp curve. He was breaking for yet another curve when he saw an old pickup truck behind him. Where did that come from?

Luna saw the truck following them as well. She had a surge of hope. Was this her chance? Andrei had slowed down for a curve. Luna opened the passenger door and dove out of the truck. She rolled and slid along on the gravel shoulder until she came to a stop. She did not hesitate; she was on her feet and running towards the old pickup, waving her arms.

Bob hit the brakes. The old truck skidded to a stop as Luna opened the door. "Por favor, ayúdame."

Bob waved her in. She was in the truck before Bob could say OK. Ahead, the white pickup had stopped. The driver was looking back at Bob and Luna. Bob grabbed his pistol and prepared to shoot. The white truck was less than a hundred yards ahead. The driver put it in gear and started backing towards them at high speed.

Bob had gotten out of the truck and was drawing a bead on the driver of the white truck. Luna stared in disbelief at the approaching truck. This was too much. She'd had enough. She started screaming, "Mátalo, mátalo, kill him, kill him." She was vaguely aware of shots being fired.

When the white truck had closed to fifty yards, Bob opened fire. It was a long shot for the 45, but he had to stop the truck. He fired rapidly, emptying all seven rounds at the truck. The rear windshield shattered as it swerved to a stop, reversed direction, and accelerated away.

As Bob loaded a new magazine into the pistol, he looked at Luna, who was sitting bolt upright, glaring defiantly at the departing white truck. She looked at him and asked. "¿Hablas españole?"

Bob got into the truck and answered. "Si, poquito solamente."

She looked frustrated. These Gringos had no Spanish. She tried to get her message across. Pointing in the direction the white truck had gone, she said. "We go—rápido, rápido. Andrei is." Here she searched for the English, giving up in frustration. She blurted, "Mal hombre."

"I know he's a bad man, but no, we are not going after him; it's too dangerous for you." Bob could see that all she understood was no, and that wasn't sitting well with her. He tried Spanish; he hoped it was correct. "No, es peligroso por tu."

Luna exploded in a torrent of Spanish with a smattering of English. Bob understood she was outraged by the thought of letting Andrei go. Peligroso or no peligroso, the man needed to be killed, she argued. He was evil. She used the phrase Seguidora de Santa Muerta.

Bob agreed with her about the man but was torn; he felt he had to get her help. He tried to change her mind. Finally, he gave up, put the truck in gear, and started after the white truck. Less than a minute had passed since he'd fired at the white truck.

+++

Bob was taking advantage of the old truck's powerful engine and pushing it as hard as the mountain road would allow. He and Luna were flying up the mountain road at way too high a speed for safety. Cutting curves to take the fastest line often put them in the wrong lane. Bob hoped no one was coming in the opposite direction.

Coming through the tight hairpin curve of a long switchback, they saw the white pickup about a quarter mile ahead. Luna pointed and said, "Ese es Andrei." Her voice was filled with hate. "Mas rápido, por favor."

As the road straightened out from the curve, Bob punched the accelerator. They were now closing fast. "Don't worry, no preocupes. He's ours." Bob wasn't worrying about catching up to Andrei; he was more concerned about what to do then. He decided that was a question to be dealt with later.

Andrei saw the old pickup following behind him. It was closing the distance quickly. He saw that it was the same truck that Luna had gotten into. The driver was some crazy cowboy who had shot part of his ear off when he tried to recover his property. Andrei was surprised to see the old pickup so close. How did he drive so fast on this road? Andrei pushed down on his accelerator. If that cowboy could do it, he could do it.

At the end of the switchback was a ninety-degree turn to the right. Andrei slowed, but not enough. His rear end broke loose, and he fishtailed back and forth across the road, finally spinning to a stop, facing the wrong direction. He could see the old truck closing fast. He turned his truck back in the right direction and mashed the accelerator to the floor.

Bob and Luna were within a hundred yards of Andrei's truck as they passed the turn-off for the Emory Pass overlook. Bob had kept up a running dialog with Luna during the chase. He didn't figure she understood much of what he was saying, but he thought it couldn't hurt. "It's downhill from here. I'm going to press him hard. He didn't show much skill going up the mountain. Downhill at speed is more dangerous."

By the second curve, Bob was on Andrei's bumper. There weren't more than twenty-five yards between the two trucks. As they entered a switchback, Bob held his distance in the approaching straightaway. Halfway through the turn, he began to accelerate. The force of the turn was almost too much, causing the tires to threaten losing traction with slight squeals and pressing Luna against the passenger door. As they cleared the curve, Bob pushed the accelerator to the floor.

Andrei couldn't believe this was happening. Looking over his shoulder, he saw the cowboy and Luna only a few yards behind. He gave his truck all the gas it had. It wasn't enough. He felt the push of the other truck. He couldn't get away from them. He started to move his foot from the gas to the brake. It was too late; he was off the road, sailing through the air to the canyon bottom.

Bob slowed down enough to see the truck hit the ground over a hundred feet below the road, flip over, and land on its roof at the bottom of the canyon. There was smoke rising from the truck, but Bob was not going to hang around long enough to see if it was going to burn. "Luna, he's dead. Let's go. Él esta muerto, vamos."

Luna asked, "¿A dónde?" To where?

Bob answered, "Home. A casa."

CHAPTER TWENTY-FIVE

Tres Cruses Ranch, Cochise County, Arizona, July 1996

Bob and Diane's family were gathered in the ranch house. Life was far from back to normal, but the tension was reduced. There was hope. Bob and Luna had arrived at the ranch two weeks earlier. The Cochise County Coroner had released the bodies of Andy and Suzie. The people of Colonia Morelos had recovered Ivan's body and brought it to Tres Cruces. Luke, Joan, and Sandra had left, carrying Andy back to Alaska for burial. Pat had had Suzie buried next to her parents in Douglas, and Luna had accepted Aunt Maria's offer and had Ivan buried next to Jack Barnes in Douglas. Ruth was to leave for Fairbanks in a few days.

Bob and Diane were in Bob's office. Diane made it clear that Luna was not going anywhere. She said, "This girl is broken. She needs time to recover. She should stay here."

Bob asked, "What if she doesn't want to stay?"

Diane said, "I already talked to her. She wants to stay. We can help her find a new start. Aunt Maria can teach her English, and we can give her a home and help her with her education. You know it's the right thing."

Bob reached out and took Diane's hand, "I know, but Baby, I'm tired, you're tired. We've been going balls to the wall all our lives. When do we rest?"

Diane squeezed his hand and said, "Rest would kill us both. A new challenge will keep us young."

"But it'll be crowded."

Diane smiled, "Is that the best you've got?"

Bob smiled, "Yeah."

"Let's go make it official."

www.ingramcontent.com/pod-product-compliance
Lightning Source LLC
Chambersburg PA
CBHW060143130626
46556CB00006B/2479